"PREDATORS HUNT THOSE WHO ARE WEAK OR STRANGE. OUTCASTS. LIKE US."

"What do you mean?" Mike asked.

"The fact that we've banded together. Plant-eaters and meat-eaters. We're defying the rules of nature," Bertram explained. "It makes us objects of curiosity and suspicion. To some, prey."

From somewhere far off, a rumbling came. Bertram looked up in alarm. Then he sighed with relief. "No storm clouds. Good. A flash flood is the last thing we need."

The rumbling came again.

"So what is that?" Mike asked, scanning the horizon but seeing nothing the least bit unusual.

The earth suddenly shuddered. The ground ahead of Mike split. A crack ran along the ground, scurrying wildly like a wagging finger.

"Earthquake!" Bertram cried.

THE TEENS TIME FORGOT

by Scott Ciencin

illustrated by Mike Fredericks

Random House 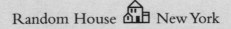 New York

To my amazing wife, Denise.
I love you, sweetheart—and literally
couldn't have done it without you!
—S.C.

www.randomhouse.com/kids

Library of Congress Catalog Card Number: 99-67551
ISBN: 0-679-88844-6
RL: 5.5

Cover design by Georgia Morrissey
Interior design by Gretchen Schuler

Printed in the United States of America March 2000 10 9 8 7 6 5 4 3 2 1
RANDOM HOUSE and colophon are registered trademarks of Random House, Inc.

Dear Reader,

Welcome to Book #2 of DINOVERSE!

If you read Book #1, you've already met Bertram Phillips, Mike Peterefsky, Candayce Chambers, and Janine Farehouse. These four eighth graders were having a typical day at Wetherford Junior High when Bertram's science fair project zapped their minds back 67 million years and dropped them into the bodies of dinosaurs.

To get back home, they must travel 250 miles, reach the Standing Stones, and unlock a mystery. So far, they've faced angry T. rexes, a raging fire, a fifty-foot crocodile, and a giant sea creature named Nessie. But their greatest challenge is still ahead.

Janine has decided to remain in the past, and without her, there may be no way for the others to return to their time—and their bodies!

You may wonder if what you're about to read is really what the age of dinosaurs was like. According to the fossil record, it very likely was. How did the dinosaurs live? What did they eat? What about the weather and landscape? All of those questions have crossed the minds of scientists. And the fossil record has given the answers to them, to me, and now to *you*.

So step into Bertram's time machine and continue your journey to a time when the world belonged not to humans, but to the most magnificent creatures the Earth ever knew.

Scott Ciencin

MIKE

Mike Peterefsky thought of himself as a simple guy. It didn't take much to please him. The roar of the crowd when he scored a touchdown. Doing well on a math test. Going to the movies. Any of those things would manage it.

But what was going on right now just wasn't doing the trick. For one thing, his tail itched. It was the middle of the night—sixty-seven million years before he'd even been born—and his *tail* was *itching*.

And for another, Mike and his companions had company. *Visitors*.

Mike swiveled his huge Tyrannosaurus head and looked around the small camp he'd made with Bertram and Candayce. There were no trees in sight. Nothing he could use to scratch his itch—except a few eight-foot-tall boulders about a hundred yards off. And the visitors Mike had detected were huddled behind those rocks.

Mike didn't have to see them to know they were

1

there. Their scent made his belly rumble.

Treading as softly as he could in his one-ton body, Mike walked over to Bertram and shook the sleeping Ankylosaurus. Bertram's club-tail rose and threatened to fall with explosive force.

"Freeze that tail!" Mike whispered. "You'll wake Candayce."

Bertram's right eye opened. Then his left. He gazed at the tiny sleeping Leptoceratops.

"What do you want?" Bertram asked. The noise the Ankylosaurus made sounded like grunts, but in Mike's mind he could hear Bertram's voice.

Bertram had explained it to them. When his M.I.N.D. Machine had sent the four of them back in time, it had turned them into pure thought-energy-brainwaves. All Mike knew was that he could talk to Bertram through his thoughts.

"Two things." Mike rubbed his tail on one of the spikes lining Bertram's back. The itch went away. "That was the first."

"Oh, good," Bertram said.

"Seriously," Mike said. "There's something here. Something new."

"Something new," Bertram repeated. "We're in the bodies of dinosaurs, being tossed every kind of threat the Late Cretaceous has to offer, and the best you can come up with to describe our current difficulty is 'something new.' I've got a bulletin for you, Mike: You're flunking the verbal portion of the exam."

Mike growled. He managed to keep himself from mentioning how it was Bertram's science fair project that had sent them back in time in the first place. Or that for a guy considered the class brain, Bertram was slow to catch on to things that were obvious to everyone else.

Yes, it *was* something new. And here, something new usually meant something *dangerous*.

"I *didn't* recognize the scent," Mike said, his razor-lined maw glinting in the moonlight. "Ergo—whatever's out there is something new."

Bertram's head bobbed. "Ergo! You actually said 'ergo.' In a sentence and everything. I'm impressed. Okay, so—predators?"

"Yeah."

"Behind the rocks, I suppose." Bertram rose on his tree-trunk legs.

"Yeah. It's the only place to hide. I must have dozed off on the watch, and they got close."

Bertram yawned. "Okay. No biggie."

Mike stared at his companion. He couldn't understand Bertram. They had already confronted a pack of T. rexes, an Elasmosaurus, and a fifty-foot crocodile. The age of dinosaurs always seemed to have something bigger, badder, or just plain *weirder* to throw at them. So acting as if this were no big deal just wasn't something Mike could do.

Cockiness'll getcha trampled, Coach Garibaldi always said. Mike had seen it happen. On the field and off.

The Ankylosaurus sighed as if he knew just what Mike had been thinking. "If they can hide behind those rocks, they're nowhere near as big as us. In case you've lost track of scale or something, you're the size of a bus, and I'm the size of a tank. *Ergo*, we can protect ourselves from anything that small."

"Raptors are small," Mike said. "But they gang up on ya."

Bertram angled his head toward the boulders. "We're not going to run into Deinonychus or any other member of the raptor family in this area or in this era. You've seen too many movies."

Sounds came from behind the boulders. Little growls. Scratching sounds.

"Something's there," Mike said. "Meat-eaters. Carnivores, like me. Those things may not want us, but we're not exactly alone here."

They both looked at Candayce.

She was curled up in her lumpy, parrot-faced Leptoceratops body, snoring. Her burns, from the forest fire the night before, were healing. Mike had a hard time picturing her the way she used to be—the blond, beautiful cheerleader and the ruler of

Wetherford Junior High's social elite.

Bertram still had a crush on her. Candayce's new thunder thighs, pot belly, and enormous backside hadn't appeared to change the way Bertram felt.

As the Ankylosaurus lifted his head, his club-tail rose again. To Mike, he looked like a knight in shining scales, ready to fight for his lady.

"They probably meant to sneak her away while we were sleeping," Bertram said. "We let her get taken from us once. It's not gonna happen again."

Mike knew Bertram felt guilty about Candayce's "abduction" by a clan of Leptoceratops. At least she'd been smart enough to survive it.

"Pincer move," Mike said. "You take 'em from the left; I'll get 'em from the right. We scare 'em off and make sure they know not to come back."

Bertram nodded.

Behind the boulders, the scratching ceased. Mike looked at Bertram. The Ankylosaurus stopped just before poking his head around the left side of the boulders. Mike was near the right side.

Mike turned the corner and sprang forward. He let let out a deafening roar! At the same instant, Bertram ran around the boulders and whacked the ground with his tail!

A handful of shapes darted forward. Their small size allowed them to pass *between* the boulders and lunge for Candayce!

"Fake out!" Mike yelled.

He saw the meat-eaters in the moonlight. They were a third of his size, with powerful rear legs, bullet-shaped bodies ending in heavy tails, long, flat skulls, and odd backward-pointing teeth.

"Theropods," Bertram said, coming out from behind the rocks. "Aublysodon, I think, or some undiscovered descendant."

Perfect time for a natural history lesson, Mike thought.

There were eight of them, all heading for Candayce. She was still out. She'd told Mike earlier that she could sleep through anything, and she'd meant it!

He saw two of the predators open their maws. Drool and spittle flew as they raced at her. They were fast and smart. The other six were splitting into two camps. They were trying to distract Mike and Bertram while the first two hauled Candayce away.

But Mike wasn't going to let that happen!

A crash sounded from behind him. Something big was rolling Mike's way.

"Veer off!" Bertram called. "I hit a boulder!"

Mike saw a blur pass him. The boulder sped like a bowling ball toward the predators, smacking into them and sending them spinning toward the earth. Then it headed right for Candayce!

"Wake up!" Mike hollered. "Candayce!"

She rolled from one side to the other. The boulder grazed the pair of predators who'd been about to attack her, then rolled harmlessly by.

Mike and Bertram chased after the predators. They disappeared into the night.

Trudging back to where Candayce lay, Mike plopped down onto his stomach. The impact made Candayce's little body flop over twice.

"Wha-what—?" she muttered, her eyes fluttering open. "Can't you guys keep it down?"

In seconds, she was snoring again.

"You're welcome," Mike said, feeling exhausted.

"I'll take the next watch," Bertram said.

"Thanks." Mike's muscles were vibrating, his own hungers and instincts still flaring. He couldn't get over the strength and speed of his new body. Soon, his heart rate slowed, and he was feeling drowsy again. Stars winked in the night sky.

He had no idea what the morning would bring. When they had started out, there had been four of them. But Janine, the acid-tongued, self-proclaimed "social commentator" of the group, had abandoned them. She had spread her Pterodactyl wings and flown away with another of her kind.

Mike hoped she was safe.

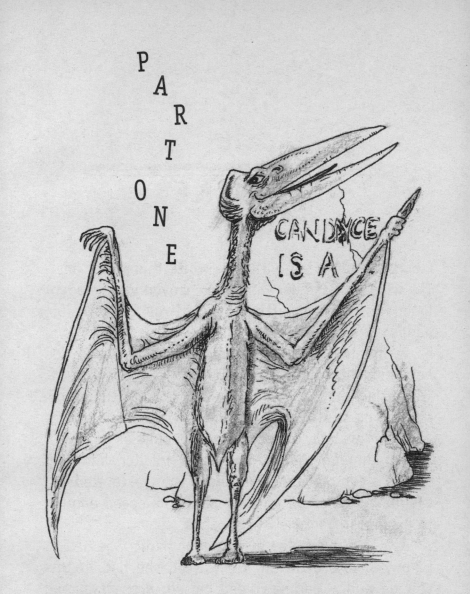

PART ONE

CANDYCE IS A

Quetzalcoatlus Quiz

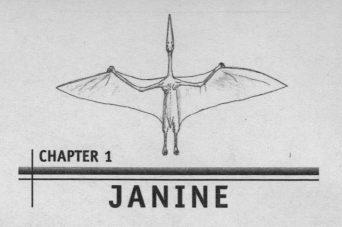

CHAPTER 1

JANINE

Clouds engulfed her with fine white tendrils of mist. The wind caressed her wings. She moved in an elegant ballet, air currents lifting her with gentle, invisible hands.

Janine flew—and it was glorious. Loki was beside her. His golden body was magnificent.

As they dropped below the clouds, she studied his rippling muscles. The streaks of gray, blue, and scarlet adorning his body suddenly became blurs as he dived. Slicing through the air, Loki grew smaller, barreling toward a copse of trees far below. Then he leveled off, caught by a draft of air that gave him speed enough to disappear from view in seconds.

Janine was gripped by a sudden panic. She had to follow. She *needed* him. He was all she had in this strange world! Janine chided herself: *Are you kidding me? Just listen to yourself!*

He'll come back, she told herself. You watch...

Janine flew lower. She saw a group of Triceratops

feeding on shrubs and playing near a pond. She saw a pair of Tyrannosaurus eyeing each other warily, their wounded prey, an Ankylosaurus, attempting to crawl away. The club-tail looked like Bertram, but she knew it wasn't him. Two days had passed since she had left the group. They'd be a good sixty miles west by now. More, considering how far *she'd* traveled.

Below, she saw a herd of hadrosaurs with three-foot-long tubelike crests on their skulls marching across a field. Mournful sounds rose up from them. Janine wondered if something was wrong—then reminded herself that she had to stop judging everything here by human standards. These Parasaurolophus weren't human and neither was she. Not anymore.

Ten miles ahead, she encountered a smaller group of hadrosaurs. The sounds from the first herd came, and they answered.

Janine got it. This was how they communicated over long distances. Like elephants. She rose higher, the clouds her destination, when a familiar cry burst from behind her.

Cawwwwwwwwwwrrrrrraaaaaaagggggggghhhhh!

Loki was back. He'd tried to make her jump by falling out of the clouds and yelling in her ear, but it hadn't worked. Janine flew in lazy circles until her companion joined her, small chirping sounds bubbling in his throat.

"What's the matter?" Janine asked. "Are you

annoyed I didn't follow? Hmm?"

Loki looked away.

"You look like my aunt Liz after she tried a cheap perm at home and all her hair fell out."

Loki cawed.

"That would have been bad enough for anyone else, but Aunt Liz was in the record books for tying one end of a rope to her hair and the other end to the bumper of a car and hauling it down Main Street. You should see the family I come from."

Loki cawed again.

"You're a font of conversation, aren't you?"

Janine plunged into a nosedive. The ground rushed up, spinning wildly. She corrected her flight, catching a pocket of thermals and using the momentum to bullet herself forward. She aimed low, flying only fifty feet above the ground, and pierced the tangled reaches of a patch of woods. The two-hundred-foot-tall Sequoiadendrons hid her nicely. She navigated the raking, snaking branches with ease.

Loki was on her tail. She led him on a terrific chase. They cruised together until Janine's stomach began to growl. Her body required so much energy that food was a constant concern. That didn't bother her. It now seemed the natural way of things.

They soared over the river, heading east to the inland sea. Loki's chosen territory. There were dangers. There were *always* dangers. But somehow, Janine didn't mind. The problems that had seemed insurmountable just days ago were behind her now.

She was rising above them in a way she had never thought possible.

Janine shrieked in absolute bliss. Loki joined her cries.

Below loomed the alien world that had become more like home to her than Montana and her mother's bed-and-breakfast ever had. Janine heard the rush of water over rocks, the howl of the river, the chirps and growls of the region's inhabitants. Closing her eyes, she felt a warmth inside her. She was at home. She was at peace.

She was happy.

CHAPTER 2

MIKE

"We can't go back," Mike growled. He was tired, hungry, and in no mood to be argued with. Bertram, his Ankylosaurus body emitting a steady stream of noxious gas, strained to keep up. Candayce walked a good hundred yards ahead.

The river had curved sharply, and following it would have taken them days out of their way. So they were cutting across the flatlands, hoping to meet up with the river farther west when it snaked back.

The view was monotonously flat. Occasionally, a hundred-foot-high ginkgo or conifer would crop up on the horizon. They'd see moss-covered rocks, berry bushes, or herbs, along with wandering herbivores made skittish by the sight of the T. rex and his companions. But that was it.

"We're never gonna find the Standing Stones without Janine," Bertram complained. "We've lost so much time, so much distance—"

"All the more reason to keep going west. We *are* going west, right?"

"I think so. If we had Janine, we'd know for sure."

Mike roared. He turned on his companion, his eyes burning, his Tyrannosaurus claws twitching.

"We *are* going west, right?" Mike hollered. "You're the one with the map buried in your head.

"Yes! We're going west! Are you satisfied? Can I *go* now?" Bertram's body tensed.

"Excuse me," Candayce called.

Mike glared at Bertram. There were things he wanted to say. It *was* Bertram's fault. If it hadn't been for him and his machine, they wouldn't be back in the Late Cretaceous, wouldn't be facing the likelihood that they were never going to get back to their own time, their own bodies.

They needed to cover close to 250 *miles*. Mike could do that in two or three days. So could Candayce. It was Bertram who was slowing them down! Plodding, methodical, pain-in-the-butt *Bertram*!

But without *him*, they wouldn't know where they were going. Mike just wanted to—

"*Guys!*" Candayce hollered. She was right in front of them now.

"We're not *moving*," Candayce said sharply. "We're not getting anywhere."

Mike felt his anger seep out of him. *And if it hadn't been for Bertram, Moriarty would have torn you apart,* he told himself, *and that croc would have had you for a midnight snack!*

"I'm sorry," Mike said. He looked ahead at the stretch of flatlands. It seemed endless. "I guess it's just getting to me."

Mike felt ashamed. He hadn't slept. Not since the night of the fire, when he'd seen footprints that he thought belonged to Moriarty. And just last night, a burst of heat lightning had lit up the sky, and Mike had seen a shape. He had tried to scent it, but his nose was still unreliable from Bertram's constant gas. So he had stared and stared at that shape, waiting for it to move, but it never did. Mike had considered rising up and challenging the shape, but he had been afraid of what might follow.

Somehow, he'd drifted off to sleep. When he woke, the shape was gone. He searched for footprints, but couldn't find any. The ground had been disturbed, and the only prints were those of Bertram.

"*Mike?*" Candayce yelled. "Are you listening?"

"Sure, right," Mike said, shaking himself out of his reverie. "We should get going."

Mike noticed that Bertram's massive club-tail was covered in dirt.

"Last night," Mike whispered. "Last night, I saw—"

"I cleared away the tracks," Bertram said in a low voice. "I didn't want Candayce to get scared."

Mike's mind reeled. Moriarty *was* stalking them.

Mike had challenged Moriarty's authority among the rexes, and the giant T. rex wouldn't stop until—

"Mike?"

Shuddering, Mike looked down.

"It's Gigantor, isn't it?" Candayce asked.

Mike stared at her. "Huh?"

"The big rex you fought. Nessie must have spit him back."

Mike and Bertram exchanged stunned glances.

"Hey," she said, "You think I don't know what's going on?"

"It could be any Tyrannosaurus," Mike said.

"Maybe," Candayce admitted.

"That *is* possible," Bertram said. "Predators hunt the weak or strange. That we're banding together— plant- and meat-eaters, defying the rules of nature— makes us objects of curiosity. To some, prey."

It wasn't any other rex, it was him, Mike wanted to say. *I can feel it.* But was his imagination running away with him?

From far off, a rumbling came. Bertram looked up. Then he sighed with relief. "No storm. Good. A flash flood is the last thing we need."

Bertram had brought up the possibility of flash floods every time there was a vague threat of rain.

The rumbling came again.

"What's that?" Mike asked, scanning the horizon.

Candayce kicked his leg. "Hello?"

Mike looked down at her. "What was *that* for?"

"I had to get your attention. We have to make a decision. About Janine."

"I thought we already—"

"No," Candayce said. "*You* decided. I say we put it to a vote."

"Janine left. She didn't want to be with us anymore. What makes you think we can talk her into coming back?"

"You don't know her the way I do," Candayce said.

Mike shook his head. "This is crazy."

"I vote we go back for Janine," Candayce said.

"I think we should keep going west," Mike said.

Candayce looked to Bertram. "It's up to you."

Bertram's head wobbled. "I—I shouldn't go. I'm too slow."

"I'm going to find her," Candayce said.

"Mike, you have to go with her," Bertram said firmly.

"Me? But—"

"She's going," Bertram said. "And I can't go with her. Do you want her going alone?"

"Of course not," Mike muttered.

"There's something I've been thinking about: The M.I.N.D. Machine took four of us. It's probably going to be searching for the same pattern for the trip back. If we give it three, instead of four—"

"You mean...if we don't go back together, none of

us may be going back at all?"

Bertram nodded. "That might be what Mr. London was—"

The earth suddenly shuddered.

"Moriarty!" Mike screamed, though he knew it was impossible. The land was flat in every direction—there was nowhere for the giant T. rex to be hiding.

The ground ahead of Mike suddenly *split*. A fissure ran along the ground, scurrying wildly. The entire world began to come apart.

"Run!" Candayce hollered, speeding past him.

"Earthquake!" Bertram cried. He scrambled in Mike's direction, but even at a scramble, he couldn't move fast enough. None of them could.

Entire shelves of earth tipped and sank into the ground like ships capsizing and sinking beneath the ocean. Ten-story-high trees were knocked down and swallowed. It was incredible.

Mike was transfixed. He felt as if he had a ringside seat at creation. A part of him understood that there was no place he could run to.

Another part wished he could be struck deaf rather than listen to the sound of the earth screaming. It was the growl of the world dying and being born...

Rock was being thrown up, the sky was filling with clouds of dirt and geysers of stone. Yet his little piece of ground was safe. It shuddered, it trembled, but it didn't fall.

Bertram had already warned him that this was the time when the Rocky Mountains were being created. Was that what was happening now?

"Mike!" Candayce screamed.

He started to turn, but something ripped out of the earth beneath him. He fell—and kept falling. The strange calm he'd known was replaced by panic.

His body struck solid rock. Pain cut through him. He bounced and spun and fell. He saw blurs of gray rock rising out of the earth as he fell, stone walls springing up all around.

He was slapped by hard stone and his fall ended, but he still felt as if he was moving. Then came a sharp crackle and a final deafening, shuddering shift of earth and stone. A wall rose higher than any sky-scraper, taller than anything he'd ever imagined.

A shovelful of darkness slapped down on him, choking him. There was pain, then the great shifting ceased, replaced with mild, timid tremors. Debris pressed in on him, and he was blanketed in silence.

Buried alive—I'm buried alive.

But Mike quickly cleared the layer of earth and stone from his face and climbed to his feet. The flat-lands were gone. In their place was a jagged shadowy valley walled in by huge flat earthen surfaces that jammed themselves defiantly toward the heavens. The air was golden with dust. Mike was trapped in this hollow.

"Mike!" came a familiar holler. Mike turned to see Bertram shambling his way. But what about—

"Up here!" Mike and Bertram looked up to see Candayce standing on a ledge far above.

"I guess that settles which of us goes hunting for Janine!" Candayce called.

Mike looked around, praying there would be no aftershocks. He could picture these walls tumbling in on them.

"Are you guys okay?" Candayce asked.

The Ankylosaurus nodded. "We're okay."

"Great. I'm outta here!"

Mike stood. "Candayce, it's too dangerous—"

"Gotta run," she said with a wave. "See ya!"

"Candayce, no!" Bertram cried.

He watched helplessly as the pudgy Leptoceratops vanished over the rim.

"So what do we do?" Bertram asked. "We've got to help her!"

Mike stared at Bertram. "She'll be all right," he said.

It was good to talk, even if he didn't believe what he was saying, because there was something else on his mind, something he had to hide from his companion: He hadn't eaten much this morning. And he was starting to feel hungry again.

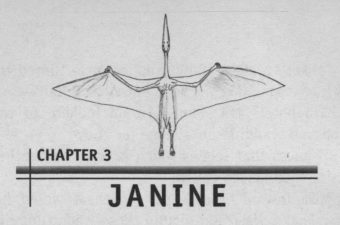

CHAPTER 3

JANINE

Janine and Loki flew with a group of Quetzalcoatlus. They circled over the inland sea, diving for small fish.

"Come on, I'll race ya!" Janine called to a smaller Quetzalcoatlus with a bright yellow body with streaks of crimson and blue. Every time he descended to snatch a fish, a larger Quetzalcoatlus stole his prize. Janine was determined to help this little guy get something to eat.

The small Quetzalcoatlus stared at her blankly.

"Okay, Bobo," Janine said to him. "I'll have to work on my nonverbal communication." She saw Loki buzz a larger flyer. Annoyed, the bigger Quetzalcoatlus snapped at Loki, then gave chase. With ease, Loki out-maneuvered the other—and sent him crashing into the flank of a third Quetzalcoatlus!

Janine soared close to the small flyer she'd named Bobo and bit him on the backside. His head came up in alarm. She sailed in again and gently whacked him on the head. His eyes became slits. She went after him a third time, but he arced around, nearly biting her! Janine fled, and Bobo soared after her.

She led the yellow-and-red flyer toward a school of radiant orange fish just below the surface of the water.

Another flyer was coming, this one with a wing-span eight feet longer than Janine's. He was going to snatch up Bobo's food! "This might be why you don't get the fish, Bobo," she said. She gave a yell, and suddenly Loki was there, distracting the incoming flyer.

With the field clear, Janine dove for the fish. As the breeze carried her up and away, she turned to see Bobo snatching a mouthful of fish, too!

She felt wonderful—until she noticed a great vibrating *ring* appear on the surface of the water. At its center, the water dipped for just an instant.

Suddenly, a giant green shape propelled itself out of the water. Janine shrieked at the camouflage-striped hide and the wide-open mouth filled with teeth. It was a Mosasaurus, the largest and most deadly lizard in history!

Janine watched helplessly as its thirty-foot torso thrust out of the water and its snout brushed the wings of Bobo. It raged higher, its jaws closing on another flyer. She heard a sharp crackling and a stran-gled cry. The flyer's eyes rolled back. The fins lining the Mosasaurus's back wriggled. Its flippers pushed at the air as if the creature was applauding its own deadly performance.

The Mosasaurus jerked back into the water as if an anchor had suddenly been thrown around its tail. It took the Quetzalcoatlus with it.

The flyers circled the quieting surface of the water. Other fish appeared. Janine watched as a few brave— or stupid—flyers snatched at them.

Loki flew to Janine's side. They broke from the group and glided to shore. Janine was still shuddering. She looked at her companion who was as unruffled as ever.

This is the way of things, Janine reminded herself. *This is the decision you made.*

She thought of Mike, Bertram, and Candayce. She laughed as she recalled the prank Loki had played on Candayce when she'd been asleep—stealing her "bikini" top. It'd been classic.

It'd *also* been nearly impossible, now that she considered things. Loki couldn't have just swooped down, severed the vine holding the shells in place, and made off with them in a single movement. Yet somehow, he'd done all this without waking Candayce. How? Did he know of a way to take off from the ground instead of vaulting off a cliff and riding the thermals?

"What about it?" Janine asked.

Loki didn't even look at her. So she cawed.

He cawed back.

Janine knew she wasn't going to get any answers this way. She wasn't certain why she'd even tried. Habit, she supposed. Thinking human thoughts, seeing things the human way, using human language—those were natural to her.

Janine wondered if she would forget what speech was like. Forget the written word altogether. Forget her family, her world...It was possible. She had no use for them anymore. And, at least as far as her family had been concerned, *they'd* never had much use for *her.*

So why couldn't she stop thinking about them?

Janine and Loki ended up on the ledge of a cliff ten miles inland. There was a deep cave burrowed into the side of the cliff. Janine had built a kind of nest there.

Her first act had been to decorate. She'd learned how to crush the garish-colored flowers into a kind of paste and use it as paint. Now the walls were covered with graffiti. She'd even carved an inscription above the mouth of the cave:

FREEDOM

Janine stared at the word. She considered what it meant. No more books. No more movies. No more *chocolate.* No more games. No more music. And what about all the conversations she'd never have?

Yeah, like the ones with Mom? "Janine, is 3A ready

yet? I don't want to hear your excuses, it's five in the morning and you haven't done a blasted thing—"

Her mom had no idea what she did at night—sneaking out, getting up the whole town with her graffiti and other stuff—like the Long Dark Night of the Soap Bubbles in the fountain near Town Hall. Her mother didn't have a clue. No one did.

Janine didn't need to brag. She kept to herself and liked it that way. People were a source of amusement, or obstacles to get around, but nothing more.

The decision she'd made was the right one. So why did she feel so down? Cawing, she bolted past Loki and leaped off the cliff. She spread her wings and waited for the invisible hands of the thermals to carry her up. They did not disappoint.

Janine heard a cry and opened her eyes. Loki was calling to her. She glided in a sharp figure eight and saw her companion—her first boyfriend, really—sailing toward the floodplains below. A low, mournful sound, like a lonely tuba, echoed from that direction. Janine followed him.

She found Loki circling over a group of Parasaurolophus inside a grove of what looked like oak and poplar trees. She'd seen these duckbills before. Their crests were long, curved affairs that bent back and away from their skulls for several feet. With them, the Parasaurolophus made the tubalike sounds.

She counted three adults, each around thirty feet

long, and four youngsters, the biggest twelve feet long. Their fat bodies were green, with pale yellow stripes down their backs and tails. At a glance, they melted into their surroundings.

Two adults walked on all fours, their thick tails straight in the air. The third stood on his hind legs and bayed at Loki.

Janine recalled that these dinosaurs were constantly wearing out their teeth. They went through twenty thousand teeth in a lifetime. She'd be grumpy if she was teething all the time, but these folks seemed to be in a good mood, despite the depressing sounds they made.

Stop trying to humanize them—they're not human, and neither are you!

They were plant-eaters. Janine wondered what Loki wanted with them. He cawed and cried, altering his course so that he was heading west.

The tuba-heads followed. Janine had seen a herd of Parasaurolophus earlier and now came upon other lost members who were using their deep bass calls to signal their location. But all of *those* tuba-heads were in the other direction!

Loki let out a yelp of triumph. He was leading them *away* from the herd, not toward it. Loki was playing another prank, like the one he'd played on Candayce.

That was one thing. Candayce had it coming. But

leading these guys astray was cruel.

Janine recalled the land to the east. Vast earthen walls would separate the herd from its lost members. The Parasaurolophus had an acute sense of smell, but those walls must have cut off their scent. Janine knew a path around the walls. *She* could lead these dinosaurs to their friends. The only thing in her way was Loki. He was leading them astray, and cackling about it in a way they couldn't recognize.

"All right, *you*," Janine said. She came up alongside him and bit his wing!

Loki was startled. Janine flew from him, recalling the sounds the herd had made. If only she could broadcast those sounds...

She closed her eyes and drifted in a lazy circle, trying hard to make silence fill her mind so she could replace it with the sounds she wanted.

A sudden stinging pain in her left wing snapped her out of it. She saw Loki drifting off, his head bobbing happily. She chased him, driving him east. Every time he tried to head in the other direction, she cut him off.

It took her a while to realize that the tuba-heads were following them. And this time, they were going the right way. Janine recalled the sounds of the herd she'd seen earlier, and *pushed* the memories into the heads of the Parasaurolophus. She also laid out a "map" and showed them how to get to their friends.

The tuba-heads trod east as Janine held Loki at bay. Once she was certain they would follow her instructions, Janine broke off, Loki behind her.

She soared happily, and he seemed to sense the change in her mood. His attitude improved as they raced to the clouds.

"We're a lot alike," Janine said. "You just need some training. Tell you what, let's go find some T. rexes and see if we can't give them some grief. Those guys *always* have it coming!"

Loki cawed happily.

Janine dove into the valley just ahead, any doubts about her decision falling away.

CHAPTER 4

BERTRAM

"We've blown it," Bertram declared. "It's over."

"What are you talking about?"

Bertram sat down hard, drawing his stubby legs under him. The walls of the mazelike chasm into which they'd been dropped were sheer, rising up a hundred feet on either side. There was no water. No vegetation. Nothing.

"We have to keep moving," Mike said. "We're hitting higher ground now. I'm certain of it."

"You scout ahead. I'll wait here."

Mike shook his head. "When was the last time you had something to eat?"

"I can't help it!"

"I'm not talking about the exhaust fumes," Mike said. "Well, actually, I am. My nose is better. I can scent pretty good right now. And that means your stomach isn't digesting. You haven't eaten. And when you don't eat, you get grumpy."

"I ate *light* this morning."

Mike nodded gravely. His stomach growled.

Bertram looked up in alarm. "You, too?"

Mike turned away. "The truth is, I was so worried about Moriarty, I didn't have much appetite. Umm...what did you mean, we blew it?"

"The Standing Stones. There's no way we can reach them in time. No way *I* can, anyway," he moaned. "And Mr. London said that I was the one who has to figure out that last thing we have to do to get home. How can I do that if I'm nowhere near the stones?"

"We're not going to abandon you," Mike said.

"If you can find a way out of this place, then you should take it!" Bertram cried. He bobbed his head morosely. "Of course, there probably is *no way*..."

"I'm not letting you go back into Eeyore mode," Mike said. "What we need is to get our minds focused on things we can do something about. Now, until Candayce comes back with Janine—"

"Never gonna happen. You're dreaming."

"Until then, we're going to find *something* for you to eat." Mike sniffed. The customary explosion of aromas and sensations entered his mind, and he sifted through them with practiced ease. "I think there're some shrubs and stuff about three miles from here. Come on."

"But if I eat, I'll pass gas, and your nose—"

"I'll survive. In fact, I smell some other stuff a few miles past the shrubs and the greens that I can eat."

"Fish? Did the river connect with all this? If it did, we could be flooded!"

"No flash floods," Mike said. "Just stuff I can eat, you know...if I have to."

Bertram decided not to push it. Besides, he and his dad had made up their minds on the "T. rex—scavenger or predator" issue. It made sense that a normal T. rex would prefer fresh meat, but would scavenge when there was none available. That was probably what Mike was going to do, and he clearly wasn't happy about it. Bertram plodded beside Mike. "Sorry I got so down."

"You're human," Mike said, tapping his tail against Bertram's flank.

They walked together for ten minutes before either spoke. Mike broke the silence. "Bertram...did you ever think about...um, this is going to sound weird..."

"You can tell me anything."

"Did you ever think about your place in things? I'm a T. rex. A predator. Predators kill to survive. When I eat fish, I'm—"

"You can't torture yourself about that."

"No, it's just...I know that fighting Moriarty to save the turtles was the right thing. But now he's after us. And what did I really change, anyway? It's the nature of things. Survival of the fittest. I know what I did was right, but sometimes I feel like it wasn't *for* anything."

The maze before them twisted and turned, and clouds drew over them from above. "Well," Bertram said, "you're probably right."

Mike stopped dead. "What?"

"Mr. London and I talked about it all the time. It's the Tree of Life. Everyone has their place. Being a predator is a natural—"

Mike walked on quickly. "Never mind."

"Wait, you don't understand—"

The Tyrannosaurus turned on Bertram with a lightning-quick twist of his neck. His eyes were wild. His maw opened.

"I'm gonna scout up ahead!" Mike roared. "Do you have any problem with that?

"I'm sorry, I—"

"Save it." Mike stomped off, growling and roaring. He turned a corner and was gone.

Bertram stood perfectly still, his mind racing. He wanted to yell something to Mike, something that would explain what he really meant. But when it came to communicating, he'd always been slow.

He didn't know how to react to Mike's flare-up. All he wanted to do was dig in and cry.

A terrible roar came from up ahead. It was more savage than any Bertram had heard from Mike in a long time.

Bertram ran as fast as he could. He turned one corner, hurried down another long corridor of stone, turned one last time—

He saw Mike standing at a dead end. A mound of stone blocked the way to the food.

"What are we gonna do?" Bertram asked, feeling tremors of fear as he looked at the Tyrannosaurus who now housed his friend. The *hungry* Tyrannosaurus.

Before Mike could answer, a sound came from above. They looked up to see another Tyrannosaurus bellowing from a ledge fifty feet up.

Moriarty. The twenty-foot-tall giant was beaten and bruised, but all too recognizable as the shadow that had been stalking them for days.

"Get away from us!" Mike screamed. "Sean, go back, all right?"

Moriarty's head swiveled, as if in confusion.

Bertram stared at his friend. "Sean? Mike, that's—"

Mike spun. "What are you talking about?"

"You called him Sean, you—"

"I didn't say that."

Suddenly, a huge rock fell in front of them, smashing and cracking at their feet. Moriarty was ripping down chunks from the loose wall of stone behind him.

"We have to go—now!" Mike said.

Bertram turned just as he heard a rumbling from above.

"Bertram, look out!" Mike yelled.

Bertram saw a shadow descending. A huge shadow. There was no time to think, no time to prepare, the boulder was upon him—

CHAPTER 5

CANDAYCE

Candayce Chambers was running for her life. This time, however, there were no carnivores chasing her.

She was running to find Janine. Running to have a chance of reclaiming the life that had been stolen from her.

Candayce charged through a shallow stream. Fallen Metasequoias stretched across the stream, leaving gaps she could duck beneath.

She wasn't sure how long it had been since she left Bertram and Mike. She had come across cracks of various sizes and widths in the earth—some only a few feet long and an inch wide, others hundreds of feet long and twenty or thirty feet wide. She didn't even want to think about how deep they were.

She pressed on, vines slapping against her shoulders and parrotlike face as she splashed through the water. Her injured shoulder still ached, and the burned areas were sore, but she ignored her discomfort. She felt the pangs of hunger and knew she'd have to stop to "gas up" soon. Something fell on her, and she screamed. It was just a vine.

Candayce drove her dinosaur body onward, her thick, round, stubby legs getting a terrific workout. She laughed inwardly. It would take a lot more than diet and exercise to do much for this body.

Still, she had to admit that being a dinosaur had some advantages. Sure, the bugs were terrible. And the smells. And all the things that wanted to chew her up and spit her out. Actually, *that* part seemed a lot like being home. But she *loved* to run. And in this body, she was as fast as the breeze and a whole lot stronger than she'd ever been before. It was also nice having all her typical pressures removed. Nice not having all her "friends" being sweet to her face while whispering behind her back, hoping she'd fail, hoping she'd do something rotten with her hair, wear clothes that were out of style, or do *something* that would give one of them the chance to be queen for a day.

Soon, the stream she was following merged with the river. The banks stretched out in a wide V shape, and even the current changed. She thought she saw something floating nearby. Probably a log, but why take chances?

She climbed onto the bank and watched as the "log" she'd just avoided opened its maw, exposing rows of jagged teeth. Some kind of croc.

Chomp, chomp, in the swamp... An old children's song came to her. A few hundred yards into the woods she found a berry bush. She leaned up against it, nibbling happily, unaware she wasn't alone.

High chirping sounds came from somewhere close. A shrill tittering. Thumps.

Screams.

Candayce abandoned her meal and plunged through the woods. She stopped at the crest of a small rise and peered down into a deep depression. What she saw horrified her.

Twelve-foot-long, seven-foot-tall ostrichlike dinosaurs swarmed around a nest. Their gray-and-gold scales glistened. Bits of shattered eggs were scattered about. She recalled Bertram's droning on about these predators. Ornithomimus. Egg-stealers.

Bertram said that many paleontologists didn't believe these long-necked, sharp-beaked creatures really plundered nests. Well, Candayce had news for them!

"Get away from there!" she screamed.

All five ostrich dinos looked up. One held a squirming baby in his beak. Candayce screamed as she launched herself at the egg thief.

Candayce was smaller than the ostrich dino, but her weight was enough to drive the screeching Ornithomimus back. As she slammed him against the hard earthen walls, the baby dino popped from his beak and scampered away. Before Candayce could do anything, another Ornithomimus swallowed it.

Candayce knocked him to the ground, staring at

the lump moving down his throat. She had to get him to dislodge it. She'd seen the Heimlich maneuver performed on TV enough times. Maybe she could—

The other egg-stealers were on her before she could even try. They clawed at her, bit her with their beaks, drove themselves at her. Suddenly, the ground began to shake.

A roar sounded from above. The egg-stealers looked at each other and scrambled out of the nest. Candayce got to her feet and kicked one of them in the backside. It kept running.

Candayce emerged from the nest, took a few wobbly steps, and saw seven *tanks* looming before her. Triceratops. Looking back at the nest, she saw the little crests on the foreheads of the babies. The Ornithomimus clan stood on one side of her. The Triceratops—their gray-and-green scales glistening, their enormous curved horns with razor-sharp tips reaching out—stood on the other.

Candayce moved, and one of the Triceratops rushed forward, then lurched to a stop. She froze.

Behind her, the egg-stealers gazed at the prizes below. It seemed that a few were entertaining thoughts of running back down there at any moment. She could picture it in her mind *so* easily.

"Don't even *think* about it!" Candayce yelled. She realized her mistake instantly. She had broadcast the images of the egg-stealers at work!

From behind her came a deafening roar. She looked

at the Triceratops. Fury was in their eyes. They'd seen the images from Candayce's mind!

"Wait!" Candayce said. "It was a mistake, I—"

The Triceratops charged. The egg-stealers ran from the nest, Candayce at their heels. The ground thundered, and Candayce looked for a way out. There was none. As the egg-stealers tried to escape, they ran in different directions. The Triceratops kept a steady line. Stampede!

Candayce ran faster than ever, but the Triceratops were gaining. They knocked down trees, trampled the ground, and roared in anger. This wasn't fair! She'd tried to *stop* the Ornithomimus from hurting the Triceratops' young! Now—

Cawwwwwwwwww! Candayce saw a pair of Quetzalcoatlus soaring over the horizon. "Janine!"

"Candayce! What are you doing?" Janine cried.

"Find me a ditch I can hide in—"

"There are none!"

Candayce heard the earth trembling. This was it.

"Turn around!" Janine yelled.

Candayce couldn't believe what she was hearing. "What?"

"Turn around and stop!"

It took Candayce no time at all to calculate how much she trusted Janine. She turned around and stopped.

The Triceratops were a dozen strong, a surging line of muscle and bone.

"Get ready!" Janine yelled.

"Get ready for what?" Candayce called.

Janine swooped, cutting in front of a Triceratops. She whipped around, pulling her wing over its eyes. Somehow the flyer managed to get the Triceratops to smash into the side of another member of the stampeding herd. With a shriek, Janine was hurled high into the air as they collided. Candayce lost sight of her in the cloud of dust that mushroomed up.

A break appeared in the line, and Candayce ran for it. More Triceratops aimed themselves at her. She saw their horns shining in the amber sunlight—and she knew it was up to her. She thought of the music she'd learned to play at her mother's parties, those dainty little piano pieces—then she quickly chose what she'd always preferred.

Candayce concentrated. Suddenly, a booming orchestra exploded all around her. It was as if the heavens had parted and all the fire and fury of the cosmos were raining down.

"Wagner," she hissed. *"Ride of the Valkyries!* Like it?"

Candayce ran between the unnerved Triceratops. She felt their shuddering flanks. Nearly screamed as they pressed against her—

And she was free! She stumbled to the ground, panting for breath. Candayce heard the roar of the Triceratops ebb. She saw the backsides of the herd as they raced after the egg-stealers. Then something slapped into her, and she tumbled to the ground, her feet caught in a twisting fistful of gnarled roots.

"Owwwwwww," she moaned, reaching for her head.

Candayce looked up and saw a tall palm tree, its sheltering branches reaching out in all directions. She'd run into a tree. A definite Smooth Move Award contender. Circling above the tree was a Quetzalcoatlus. It wasn't Janine. The colors were all wrong.

"Janine!" Candayce yelled. She saw a figure lying on the ground, a dark crimson body with bright blue wings. *"Janine!"*

The fallen figure did not answer.

CHAPTER 6

MIKE

Mike watched in horror as the heavy boulder fell toward Bertram. But before the rock could flatten him, his tail whipped around and *smashed* it to pieces.

Mike was stunned—and impressed.

A few more stones tumbled down. Mike saw Moriarty struggling to free more debris.

"Bertram, come on!" Mike called. "It won't be so easy if he's got a moving target!"

Bertram looked over. "I got it, didn't I?"

"You sure did."

Bertram moved as fast as he could. They back-tracked along the deep channel. Above, Moriarty roared in frustration. He followed, showering them with rocks whenever he could. Bertram, unable to move swiftly enough, took the worst of it.

Mike decided he had to do something about that.

"Hey, butt-crack breath!" Mike yelled, waving his little arms and hopping in place. "It's *me* you want, stupid. I'm right here! Come on!"

Moriarty turned his full attention on Mike, sending rocks down upon the teenage T. rex. Mike darted and danced, only occasionally getting struck by falling debris.

"You really think what I did was good?" Bertram asked timidly. "Smashing the rock with my tail?"

"If it was baseball season, I'd put you on my team any day!" Mike wheezed.

"You'd be the first."

"I mean it!" Mike dodged another rock. It exploded beside him. He kept hoping Moriarty would run out of ledge, but it didn't seem to be happening.

Mike looked at Bertram's raised tail. Then he saw the rocks lying at their feet. "Hey, Bertram, how about a little batting practice?"

Mike knelt with his legs and bent forward, pressing his head against the wall to keep himself from falling flat. His small but immensely powerful arms picked up a boulder. It was a good two feet around.

"Mike, what are you doing?"

"I'm the pitcher, you're at the plate."

"What?"

Mike tossed the boulder at Bertram's tail. Bertram whacked the rock so hard it shattered. Mike had to duck to avoid the explosion of stone pieces!

"Once more, just lighten up a little." Mike said, grabbing another rock. "You want to make the ball go on a little trip, you don't want to pulverize it."

He tossed the "ball."

Bertram swung! There was a sharp *crack*, and the rock became a blur. It smacked into the wall, leaving a small crater. But at least it stayed in one piece.

"Not bad!" Mike said. He saw Moriarty watching them in confusion. Good. At least he had forgotten his own little game.

"You're a natural, Bertram. When we get back—"

"If we get back—"

"*When* we get back, you and me are gonna do some serious practicing, you got that?"

"*Really?*" Bertram asked.

"Darned straight. Here comes the pitch!"

Bertram whacked the boulder. It sailed straight up and landed to Mike's right. "Fly ball. It happens."

Mike grabbed another rock and tossed it.

This is the one, Mike thought. *I can feel it...*

Bertram's tail smacked into the rock at just the right angle. It flew at Moriarty as if it'd been launched by a catapult!

The rock hit Moriarty square in the forehead! He rocked back, legs buckling.

Mike tossed another stone. *Whack!* Mike laughed as it struck Moriarty in the stomach. Another—and it struck his knee. Moriarty roared and fell, his tail hanging over the cliff. Another pitch—and Moriarty, who'd gotten to his feet once more, took it on the jaw. He fell with a thunderclap that caused an entire shelf of

rock to rain down on Mike and Bertram.

Once the dust had cleared, Mike knew that Bertram was okay. He couldn't see Moriarty.

"Home run!" Mike yelled.

"Oh, yes! Oh, yes!" Bertram bellowed. He happily bounced from side to side, bobbing his head.

"You're a heckuva guy!" Mike hollered.

"Me?" Bertram asked.

"You the man!"

"*Who* the man?"

"You the man!" Mike shook his head. "I wouldn't

want to be here with anyone else."

"You mean it?"

"Sure." Mike's stomach growled. Bertram turned back to the path leading to the food.

"Mike, look!"

Mike saw that a ramp had been formed by the last round of falling rock. It led up the wall of debris that blocked them from the food.

"I'll race ya," Mike said, but he saw that Bertram looked troubled. "What?"

"I'm sorry about before. I didn't mean it the way you took it. About being a predator, and that what you did on the beach didn't mean anything."

Mike hung his head. "Bertram, there's something I should tell you. It's something I'm not proud of. And once you hear it, you might not think of me the same—"

Bertram shook his head. He didn't look as if he was listening. "All I was trying to say is that to a predator, a *real* predator, what you did wouldn't mean anything. But that's not what you are. Just because you're in that body doesn't make any difference as far as who you *really* are. What you did was right for you. It was the most incredible thing I've ever seen. If you had to do it again, you would. That's what makes you better than Moriarty."

"But the killer instinct," Mike said.

"You do what you have to do to survive. Moriarty was hurting those turtles because he liked it. Like he was better than everybody else. Believe me, Mike, I've been dealing with predators all my life, and you're not one of them. You're better than that. You are."

Mike didn't know what to say.

"What'd you want to tell me?" Bertram asked.

Mike shook his head. "Not now." He needed time to think about everything Bertram had said. And what he would do *if* and *when* they got back.

Mike looked up at the cliff where he'd last seen Moriarty. He wanted to believe this was the end of it, that Moriarty would leave them alone. Somehow, though, he knew that wouldn't be the case.

Then he looked at Bertram and thought, *We'll be ready for you.*

And for the first time since he'd glimpsed the giant T. rex on the beach, Mike was no longer afraid.

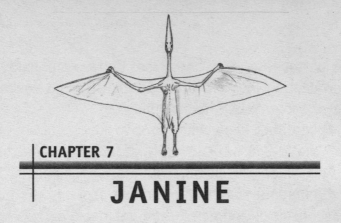

CHAPTER 7

JANINE

Janine was shaking her head, trying to get the sound of the thundering herd out of her ears, when Candayce descended on her. The other girl was all flashing hooves and licking tongue, snapping beak and rolling eyes. "Are you okay? Are you—"

"Get, get, *get!*" Janine snapped.

"I'm so glad you're all right," Candayce said as she scrambled back. "That was *amazing!*"

Janine stretched her wings and stood. "Do you know how close that thing came to ripping my wing?"

"Never seen anything like it," Candayce said. Her eyes looked teary. Maybe it was sweat.

Janine couldn't handle this. "Is there a *reason* why I'm looking at your ugly...little...*face?*"

Candayce drew back as if she'd been slapped. Her eyes became hard. "Okay, I had that coming."

A lot more than that, Janine thought.

"We need you," Candayce said. "We're not gonna make it if you don't come back."

"Give me a break."

"There was an earthquake. Didn't you feel it?"

Janine nodded. She'd seen the earth tremble.

"The ground—it, like, opened up and swallowed Mike and Bertram. They're trapped. It's a maze down there. It went on for miles. We have to help them!"

"You're serious."

"You can help guide them out."

Janine was silent. "You *are* serious..."

"Please," Candayce whispered. "You can't just—"

"Don't tell me what I can and cannot do!" Janine screeched. Above, Loki wailed and circled, agitated.

"You're right, okay? I'm sorry. I'm just..."

"You're just *what?*"

Candayce didn't answer.

"I asked you a question."

Candayce turned away. "I hadn't even...I didn't consider that you might say no."

Janine was stung. She hadn't said no. She hadn't said *anything* yet. She was too busy trying to take it all in. Janine asked, "Are they hurt?"

Candayce shook her head.

"Thank goodness for that much, anyway."

"Janine—"

"Let me think!"

Candayce dropped onto her side and looked as if she might start sobbing at any moment.

Don't be so pathetic, Janine thought. She knew she

was being cruel, but all she could think about was the time she'd begged Candayce to be nicer to Bertram—and Candayce swore to torture the poor guy for caring about her.

Janine heard Loki caw. "Give me a minute, I'm thinking."

"I didn't *say* anything!" Candayce wailed.

"Not you."

Candayce looked up at the Quetzalcoatlus circling above. "Oh. You can understand him."

Better than I can understand you. Janine shook her long head. "It just had to be *you*, didn't it?"

Candayce looked at Janine. "What?"

"It couldn't have been Mike. No, it had to be *you* asking."

"Mike's—"

It came to Janine suddenly. "Now I get it! Without them, *you* can't get back. That's why you're worried!"

Candayce's eyes narrowed. For a moment, her shoulders tensed, then the fight drained out of her. "Okay...okay, if that's what you want."

"I was just trying to figure out why you looked so concerned," Janine said. "For a minute there, I actually thought you had it in you to be worried about someone else. Now it makes sense."

"Janine," Candayce said softly, "will you..."

"Of course I'll do it."

Candayce's eyes widened. "You will?"

"Yes."

"Good. Wonderful. Thank God." Candayce tromped her way excitedly.

"Stop!" Janine hollered.

Candayce froze.

"Don't gloat. Don't even—I swear—"

"Gloat? I—"

"One more word, *one more word* out of you and I'll stay here and that's the end of it. I mean it."

Candayce got to her feet and tensed like a new recruit at boot camp. Janine waited for a minute, and Candayce remained eerily silent.

"I can't believe this. I've finally shut you up."

Candayce looked away. Janine could sense the anger within her companion, but that was all right.

"You know what?" Janine asked. "This'll be worth it. Just to have the chance to say all the things I've wanted to say to you. Yeah, this'll be worth it."

They walked until they found a hillock. Janine launched herself into the air. Candayce ran below her. They traveled through an open area with only a few trees. Janine wanted to to keep an eye on Candayce.

Soon, rumbling sounded from far off. Was it thunder? Another earthquake?

Fear twisted Janine's insides into a knot. She thought of Mike and Bertram being buried beneath the rocks. No, she had to think about something else. "So, Chambers!" Janine cried. "Remember the day we met? *Don't answer that!*"

Candayce didn't say a word.

"I remember. My mother had made a brand-new dress for me. I was on the bus. Fourth grade. We'd just inherited the bed-and-breakfast and come back to town, and my mom wanted me to make a good impression. I guess you picked up on that. I remember you and your friends coming over, acting so nice...That was when I looked down and saw that you'd just opened your pen all over my dress. Everyone got a good laugh."

Candayce ran, head down. Janine soared above, wondering why this wasn't more fun...

"Then there was Sherilyn. Remember her? My best friend until sixth grade. Then you guys started being nice to her, and the next thing I knew, it was a Monday morning and Sherilyn started hitting me. I couldn't believe it was happening. I went down *hard* and saw you and your thugs standing around, laughing, making jokes. Sherilyn told me she didn't have time for a loser like me.

"But I bet you don't know what she did later. She came over after school that day. She said it didn't mean anything. Her beating me up. She said it was just to impress you. But we could still be friends, so long as we didn't go anywhere where anyone'd see us. Isn't that *classic?*"

The rumbling came again. The day was deepening, and clouds were moving in. Loki sailed close. His wings nearly grazed Janine's. "Hey!" she yelled with a piercing shriek. He veered off, straining in the direction of the clouds. The rumbling came again.

"What're you, scared of a little rain?" Janine asked.

Janine liked the rain. When she was still human, she'd looked forward to rainy days. Everyone at school was too busy being miserable over the weather to get on *her*. She heard the rumbling again.

"Hey, Chambers, you're off the hook for a while. We've got some weather up ahead."

Candayce loped on, nodding at Janine.

Janine shook out her wings. "This wasn't any fun, anyway. You probably didn't listen to a word I said..."

Candayce was no longer looking Janine's way.

They traveled for hours. The sky remained bleak, the thunder a phantom they appeared to be chasing. Janine had been tempted to pick up her little tirade, but recounting all the hurts Candayce had caused wasn't doing her any good.

She could have cursed and screamed and called Candayce Chambers every name she could think of, and it wouldn't have mattered. This was just—old tapes. Old tapes that needed to be erased. And once she made sure Mike and Bertram were all right and safely on their way, she'd forget the life she'd led...

If only the silence hadn't been so terrible.

She hadn't noticed it before. Not when she was talking *at* Loki. She had really felt it only in the last few hours. She *missed* talking. She couldn't help but think of all the conversations she would never have once Mike and the others were gone.

"Candayce," Janine called.

The running Leptoceratops didn't answer.

"Chambers, hey!"

Still no reply, just an upward glance.

"You can talk now. It's all right."

Candayce nodded, then looked away. The thunder sounded, louder now. Closer. Janine didn't notice. "Look, all that stuff before...it just doesn't matter, all right?"

Silence. Rolling in. Beating on her.

"Didn't you hear me? I said—"

The silence was shattered by a savage crackling and a brilliant flash of blinding white fire. Janine felt the air around her become fired with agonizing little lances of vibrating terror that ripped through her.

She smelled something burning, and her head went numb. She could remember how to fly, but she was falling even as the pain was subsiding. She was falling, and an image came to her, a moment from that other life.

It was the day her father had helped her fly her first kite. She saw the kite whipping around in the sky. Then it fell, and she thought for a moment of what it must have looked like from the kite's view as the green earth rose up. The kite struck, crackled, and broke.

Now she didn't have to imagine. The ground pummeled her, and her arm twisted beneath her. She heard Loki screeching and Candayce wailing. Little drops of rain tapped her face as she tumbled to a jarring, nasty stop.

"Janine!" Candayce shouted. *"Janine!"*

Shaking, Janine tried to clear her head and force herself up, but something was wrong. Her right claw grasped the earth, yet when she put pressure on it, nothing happened. There was just a wobbling, and she didn't understand...

"Lightning—the lightning hit you, Janine!"

Then Candayce was helping her, and Janine was sitting up, and her arm and her wing lay at an odd angle, folded in a way that was impossible, that was wrong. Then, as words from a children's rhyme came into her head, she knew.

Little wing, broken wing...

She knew.

CHAPTER 8

CANDAYCE

Candayce stared at Janine's twisted wing and knew there was no hope of helping Mike and Bertram, no hope of getting home. They were trapped here.

These thoughts were quickly replaced by more urgent concerns. Candayce knew they could not stay here. There was no protection from the storm. No tall trees to draw the lightning. They were out in the open.

"You've gotta get up," she said. "You don't need your wing to walk."

A clicking came from Janine. Her beak.

"I can't drag you." Candayce held out her hooflike claws. "See? I would if I could."

"Go away."

"It's not safe."

"Not safe anywhere," Janine muttered. "Stupid."

"It doesn't look that bad!"

Janine's long beak tilted toward Candayce. "It doesn't?"

"Look," Candayce said.

Janine shuddered. "Bad enough."

"I don't know *anything* about first aid. I don't know how to recognize if someone's in shock. I—"

Janine snapped her beak, almost biting her. Candayce drew back, trembling. "So you're just gonna wallow in it," accused Candayce.

"Stuffed," Janine whispered, hugging her bent wing to her as if it was a sick child as the rain poured down. "Get stuffed, you selfish little—"

Candayce backed off. "I don't need this. I don't have to listen to you."

"Good. Go."

Candayce went a few yards, and stopped. She was waiting for Janine to call her. But she didn't.

Candayce went back anyway. She knelt in front of Janine. She waited. Janine finally looked up. Candayce snagged her beak in her claws.

"What are you doing?" Janine cried.

Candayce leaned in close, staring into Janine's frantic eyes. "You know what I'm doing. You've done it to me enough times." Candayce didn't know how to *look inside* someone, but she was counting on Janine's being too upset to consider that. Janine raked at Candayce with her good claw, but the Leptoceratops ignored the blows.

"I see what your problem is," Candayce said. She'd known it before she even returned for the wounded flyer. Janine stopped struggling. She opened her mouth—and exhaled. A foul smell attacked Candayce. "Fish breath, gah!"

Candayce released Janine. The Quetzalcoatlus sprang up on her back legs and eyed Candayce warily. A caw drifted down from the hissing rain and moaning winds. Janine looked up. Loki stared down at her. Lightning bruised the clouds and lit his face. He looked different, somehow. He appeared stony, removed.

Candayce knew that look. She knew it all too well.

"Loki?" Janine said. Her voice almost broke.

With a flash of his wings, Loki sailed north, disappearing into the darkness in seconds.

"Don't!" Janine called. "Don't go..."

Candayce felt horrible. She hadn't expected any of this. "He's not coming back," she told Janine.

"What are you *babbling* about?"

"Guys. I know what it means when they give you that look."

"He's a Quetzalcoatlus! Not some *guy*."

"That look means you're damaged goods. You're not desirable anymore."

"I'm sure *you've* had guys look at you like that."

Candayce shrugged. "This is me you're talking to. If they gave away prizes for every time you steal someone's boyfriend just because you *can,* how many do you think I'd have?"

Janine waited. "You're scum. I know that."

"That's the look. That's the look they give the one they're leaving behind."

"No."

"No?"

"He'll be back," insisted Janine.

"Okay. So, until then, come on, let's go."

"Get *away* from me! This is all your fault!"

"You bet."

"I wouldn't have been flying this way, wouldn't have been out in this if—"

"Right. I'm the bad guy. I'm used to that. I know all about it. Now can we leave here?"

"*You* leave."

Candayce looked up. The rain was getting worse, and in a way, that was a comfort. Her summers in Cocoa Beach had taught her that the most dangerous time to be out in a storm was just before it really opened up—and just after. The times when it looked calm were the most threatening. The lightning was more likely to get you then.

"I'm not going anywhere," Candayce said.

"The lightning."

She thought of the Leptoceratops she'd seen struck by lightning several nights earlier. It'd been a horrible sight. "It gets both of us or it doesn't get either of us."

"Bull."

"Hey, I'm here, aren't I?"

Janine's beak darted about crazily as she searched

for a reply. "I hate you!"

"I hate you, too, but I'm still not going anywhere."

Janine fell on her tailbone. "Haven't you done enough?"

"I want you to understand that you don't know everything."

"What?"

The rain was freezing. Lightning flashed, and Candayce saw it rip apart a tree. "That was *close*."

"So go."

"No. Like I said, I want you to understand—"

"I wish you were dead."

"Sure."

Janine shook. *"Stop agreeing with me!"*

"Maybe. One condition."

"What?"

"You and I, we play the Quiz. We play, then I go. You follow or you don't." Candayce waited.

Slowly, Janine nodded.

"Playing is simple. All you have to do is tell the truth. You remember what that's like, right?"

"Ask your question."

"Do you have any idea why I'm so afraid of you?"

Janine looked startled. Her wide eyes sparkled in the dim light of the storm. "What?"

"That's not an answer."

Janine thought. "Because I don't want to be like you. Because I don't care what you think of me. You can't control me. You can't get to me."

"That's part of it."

Janine took a step forward. Her back straightened. She loomed over Candayce, which seemed to make her feel better. "So what's the rest?"

Candayce wanted to keep her mouth shut. She had driven herself into this trap, laid herself out, and *knew* the whole time where it was heading. And she did it anyway.

Janine was right. She was an imbecile.

"I admire you," Candayce said in a strangled voice.

"What?"

"I wish I was more like you."

"I am gonna kick your—"

"It's true. You've got integrity." Candayce spoke so softly the rain nearly swallowed up her words.

"Say that again. I'm not sure I heard you right."

"You wouldn't stab a friend in the back just to get a date." Candayce's chest heaved. Her words faltered. "I was always scared...that you really *could* look inside people. Scared you'd see—"

"Shut up!"

Candayce drew back. "I can't be like you. You don't know what it's like. What they expect out of me. It's like, I don't even sleep at night, not really. It's why I'm in therapy. It's why I have to punch things, the tae kwon do, the kickboxing, why I can't do anything right on the piano, 'cause I'm too busy slamming the keys, why I can't ever tell anyone—"

"You selfish little *witch!*"

"I'm telling you the truth! Ask me—"

"It's always got to be about you, doesn't it? You expect me to feel sorry for you? *You made my life hell!*"

Candayce hugged herself. "I know."

"You just can't stand it, can you? You can't stand that I'm out here, and everything I want is here, and I'm happy, and you can't stand it!"

"I—"

"You just have to take! You have to take and take

and—you don't know anything about me!"

Lightning tore across the sky. "You don't know everything. You only think you do."

"I know what you are."

"*I know what you are, too!*" Candayce screamed. The downpour lessened, the thunder softened, and suddenly, there was only a thin wall of drizzle separating her from Janine. Candayce knew she was crying, even though she couldn't tell if tears were really falling or not. She could feel a sharp, biting cloud of regret and sorrow easing from her. She didn't want Janine to be able to hurt her again.

"You know what I am. What am I?" asked Janine.

"Your mother knows."

Janine stiffened. "She knows what?"

"Your mother knows. I know. Everyone knows."

"What are you talking about?"

"What you do at night. Your mother knows you go out and deface property. Your graffiti. She *knows*."

Janine cradled her wounded wing. "No..."

"Who do you think has to pay for it every time they paint over what you've done? Why do you think your mother never has any money? It's because she's spending it cleaning up after you. Those days when she's not around and you have to stay home from school and work, where you do think she is? She's trying to keep you from getting busted, she's—"

"You shut up!"

Candayce sat down wearily. "You call *me* selfish.

You're out there every night, because—what? Your mom doesn't pay you any attention? I should have your problems. Your mom doesn't talk to you because she doesn't know what to say. She's afraid you'll run off if she confronts you. She's afraid you will, anyway. And I guess she has pretty good cause for feeling that way, *don't you?*"

Janine folded herself up and sat down across from Candayce. "She knows?"

Candayce nodded.

"How can you say you *admire* me, then say *that?*"

Candayce didn't answer right away. "I don't know. Maybe it's because you always do what you want, no matter what, and I do what people tell me. You do the things I'd be too afraid of doing."

Janine stared at her with unblinking eyes.

Candayce felt tired. "Not everybody knows. My mom knows because she's one of the officers at the bank. She doesn't *want* it getting out. And I won't say anything. Not to anyone."

"Sure you won't."

"I *haven't*. And I've known for a long time."

Janine stared at the ground. "Mom knows?"

"Yeah."

"Everything."

"Uh-huh."

Janine looked into Candayce's eyes. "Even about the fountain?" Janine asked.

"The fountain?"

"That time I put all that pink bubble bath in the fountain across from Town Hall. It was in the papers. You should've heard my mom going on about it, she was so mad. I never understood why that would make her mad, but—"

"That was *you?*" Candayce yelped.

Janine leaned forward, excited. "You didn't know?"

"No. But...that was funny."

Candayce hesitated. "Why'd you do it? Why'd you do any of it?"

"Why'd you make Sherilyn hate me?"

Candayce looked at Janine. Small, chirping, bubbling sounds were rising from inside her. Sobs. She didn't want to cry. She wouldn't cry. She wouldn't.

As the rains finally stopped, Candayce found herself moving until Janine rose up before her, her left wing spreading, enfolding her. Candayce hid herself in the welcoming darkness and cried until she ran out of tears.

She wasn't alone.

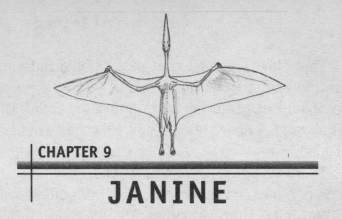

CHAPTER 9

JANINE

They walked for hours, wet, cold, desperately in need of sleep, and each terrified of what the other might say. Janine refused to stop, refused to sleep, refused to consider all that Candayce had told her. They ate, stuffing themselves, then trudged on.

"I'm worried about Mike," Candayce said finally.

"Me, too."

"And Bertram. I mean, what if Mike loses it? If he can't find anything to eat? I should've brought them food. I didn't think."

Guess not, Janine considered. But she didn't say it.

They walked until pale slivers of silver and blue appeared on the horizon. Janine saw treetops—beech and maple. Heard the sound of the river. Smelled herbs.

"We should be close to where Mike and Bertram fell," Candayce said. "I mean, relatively."

For some reason, Janine didn't think so. This was more like the floodplains—

Suddenly, the ground rumbled. Janine and Candayce fell together. Trees toppled. The earth moaned and crashed and—

It was over.

Candayce's body was wracked with tremors. "We're so close to Mike and Bertram. That earthquake might have buried them!"

Janine placed the claw of her good wing on Candayce's back and guided her forward. A dim gray light washed over the woods. Sounds rose, and shapes scurried about in the darkness. Two shapes were enormous.

"Not T. rexes," Candayce whined.

"Shhhhhhhh!"

The shapes moved off in the other direction. A shaft of sunlight leaped between the thick covering of maple leaves and struck them. Janine saw curving horns and elephantlike bodies. "Triceratops," she whispered.

Candayce hugged the ground. "No rexes. Thank you, thank you..."

"The river's off to the right. I can hear it," Candayce said.

"The right?" Janine was disturbed. It should have been off to their *left*. Had the minor quake they'd experienced opened a branch to the other side of them? Were they trapped?

"We should keep to the shallows, the way I did when I was looking for you. It'll throw off our scent, and we won't leave tracks and—"

"Yeah, maybe." Janine was too busy studying the terrain to really listen.

They walked on, passing between a pair of towering Metasequoias. Janine saw the river. It wasn't some newly made branch. It was the river she'd flown over for days.

She sat down hard. "We got lost. We went around in a big circle. Look." Janine pointed away from the river, toward a group of Triceratops gathered around a host of fallen trees. They were a good distance off. "Look familiar?"

"The Triceratops?"

"Not just Triceratops. The *same* Triceratops."

Candayce looked to the river, then said, "I'm tired."

Janine felt herself becoming calm, just as she had when she'd first entered this prehistoric world, falling to what should have been her death. "We need to sleep. You go first, I'll watch. Then we'll switch. After that, we'll start over."

"Okay." Candayce looked at the Triceratops. A strange expression came over her face. *"The nests."*

Candayce started off in the Triceratops' direction. "Are you crazy? What are you doing?" Janine said.

"The nests..." It was all Candayce would say.

Janine followed. "They won't let you *near* the nests."

Candayce kept going. "They won't hurt us," she

said as she drew closer to the herd.

"Really?" Janine stared at the Triceratops and wished she could believe that. A throbbing pain began in her wounded arm, which had been numb until now.

Little wing, broken wing...

Janine stopped. Candayce kept going.

Janine saw Candayce awkwardly pick up something in her claws. She cradled it and kept walking.

Was that an egg? Janine wondered. *An egg that had rolled from the nest during the tremor? How could Candayce have known?*

Little wing, broken wing, fly in your heart, soar in your soul, believe that all things are possible, and you will be made whole...

Janine went after Candayce.

Candayce walked between a pair of Triceratops. They regarded her with dark, sad eyes. She nodded, then lowered her gaze and walked past them.

Janine approached slowly.

One of the Triceratops glared.

She nodded toward Candayce. "I'm with stupid."

The Triceratops grunted and turned his attention back to the Leptoceratops.

Sure, Janine thought. *Why should they be afraid of me? I'm wounded. If I get out of line, they can stomp me.* It wasn't a comforting thought.

She caught up with Candayce at the rim of the nest. The ground had torn itself open at the lowest point. It now looked more like a well. Branches and bits of rock led down into the darkness, and a handful of eggs lay perched on a small ledge a dozen feet straight down. Beyond that lay a pool of river water.

Peering into the depths, Janine saw that the eggs were caught in a netting of tangled roots.

She saw Candayce gently setting the egg she'd found before one of the Triceratops. She backed away from the treasure. The egg had a small crack on one side, but was otherwise perfect.

The Triceratops gathered around the egg.

"We have to get the others," Candayce said.

Janine glanced into the chasm again. "I don't see how."

Candayce walked over to a Triceratops and rubbed the side of her face against his neck. Then she tugged gently on his tail. He took a lumbering step backward, then another.

After a few more steps, Janine saw Candayce motioning for the Triceratops to stop. But it didn't appear to understand, so Candayce sat down behind it, near the edge of the well.

"This is nuts! *Candayce*—"

"He won't hurt me."

The Triceratops lifted its leg, brought it down inches above Candayce—and stopped. Looking over its shoulder, the Triceratops squinted at Candayce. The leg moved forward, then came down with a thunderous *bang*.

Janine sighed with relief.

Candayce turned over onto her belly. She wrapped her pudgy but powerful legs around the Triceratops' leg and awkwardly climbed, face first, into the pit. She stretched out her arms, dislodging earth and stone. A few rocks hit either side of the eggs, then skipped down to the water with a splash. Candayce couldn't reach the eggs on her own.

"Your turn!" Candayce called.

"Wait a minute," Janine said. "My arm, it's—"

"You're hollow-boned. Light. I'll hold your leg with my mouth. You scoop the eggs up with your beak, one at a time."

Janine thought of all the ways this could go wrong.

Believe...

She eyed the Triceratops. It was one thing for the creatures to trust Candayce. She had brought them one of their eggs. But Janine was a predator. And she was hungry. They'd probably scented her hunger already. Being here was crazy! Yet when she glanced back at the eggs, she knew it was right.

"Okay," Janine said. "I'm going to lower my leg to you. *Don't bite down.*"

"Right."

Janine pushed an idea into Candayce's thoughts. Candayce, who'd been mountain climbing half her life, parried with a few ideas of her own.

"Cool," Janine said, amazed that she and Candayce

had been able to agree on something.

Janine then turned to face the Triceratops who was acting as Candayce's brace. Her back was to the abyss.

"All right, McGurk," she said. "Don't move. If you move, bad things could happen. So *don't move.*"

The Triceratops didn't even look her way. "Good, McGurk."

Janine drew a deep breath and slowly unfurled her wings. Her wounded arm exploded with pain as she tried to straighten it. She pulled it back, keeping it slightly bent. Taking another breath, she hugged the wall and lowered her feet down to Candayce. She struck something hard. A rock maybe.

"Ow!" came a cry from below.

"What?"

"That was my head."

"Sorry," Janine said. *Mostly.* She lowered her feet a little more. Candayce chomped down on her left ankle.

"Hey!" Janine wailed.

Candayce eased up on the pressure.

"Better," Janine said. She dug her claws into the earthen wall.

Slowly, Janine secured her left claw to the side. Then she brought her right over and found a hold with it. Her ankle moved a little in Candayce's mouth, and she used her other foot to dig a foothold. She thought of geometry classes and how she had wondered what possible use any of these lessons could be in the real world.

Now she knew. *She* was the protractor.

Candayce held Janine's ankle firmly, but with the right amount of give. Janine crawled along the earthen wall as if she were the hand of a clock moving backward. Soon her long beak and her spine faced eleven o'clock. Ten. She kept crawling. Eight o'clock. Seven...

The eggs came into view. Janine had to strain to reach. She opened her beak carefully, closed it over one of the eggs, tested for just the right amount of pressure, and lifted it out. The egg was heavier than she'd expected, but somehow she held on to it. She started the long climb back to the surface. Eight o'clock. Nine. Ten...

As the rim of the pit came into view, Janine saw a conference of Triceratops gazing down at her like scientists observing an experiment. Their horns glinted in the harsh sunlight. McGurk was holding still. He'd only moved back a few feet—apparently to make room for the newcomers.

Janine raised the egg over the top of the rim, her beak poking out and away from the pit. She opened it, and the egg rolled to the foot of a Triceratops and stopped.

Janine's right wing was killing her.

Five to go.

Janine worked for close to thirty minutes and managed to retrieve the next four eggs without much difficulty.

"You doin' okay?" she asked Candayce.

The Leptoceratops grunted.

Janine went back for the last egg. She was at ten o'clock when a flaring pain ripped through her right arm. Her wing twitched and straightened involuntarily. It whipped outward and caught a breeze. Janine gasped as she was torn free of the earthen wall. She spun back, certain that the ankle Candayce was holding would be ground to dust in the Leptoceratops's grasp.

Instead, Candayce held on, tight enough to keep her from falling, but loose enough that her ankle moved in Candayce's mouth like a ball in a socket. Janine cried out as she saw the opposite wall, then flipped again and *slapped* into the wall she'd been climbing. She dug in with her other foot.

Her arm was killing her, but there was still one more egg in the nest. She had to concentrate on that one. Carefully, she moved to capture it.

Chest heaving, she called, "Okay, haul me out of here!"

Nothing happened.

Favoring her wounded wing, she found holds off to her left and scrambled. Eleven o'clock. Ten...

The walls shuddered. She looked up and saw exactly what she didn't want to see.

McGurk was dangling one tree-trunk leg over the side of the earthen wall. Candayce was still attached to it, her legs clamped around his, her eyes squeezed shut, her body trembling with exertion and agony. But she didn't let go—and she didn't bite down, because that would have meant crushing Janine's leg.

Janine was stunned. The wall was collapsing under McGurk's weight!

Janine reached out with her hurt wing. She stretched it to full length and clawed at the earthen wall. She sent an image into Candayce's mind of the Leptoceratops releasing her. The return mail was a wave of panic. Still, Candayce opened her mouth, and Janine yanked her leg free. Trembling, Janine dug both feet into the wall, then extended her bad arm.

Fiery lances of pain ripped through her, but she gripped with her right, then hauled up her good arm and clawed a firm hold, then did it again, and again, until the rim of the pit loomed. She whipped her beak over the top and opened it, allowing the egg to roll free. Then she climbed out of the pit.

Janine flopped onto the ground and laughed with relief, spreading her wings—

And striking McGurk.

Candayce!

Janine got to her feet. McGurk was leaning back over the edge of the pit, his hind leg dangling over the rim. Janine gazed into the darkness to see Candayce.

"Hold on!" Janine cried. "Just hold on!"

McGurk's other foot was halfway over the rim. The ground beneath it was giving way. Most of his weight and part of his massive rump were centered on the limb dangling over the abyss. His tail flopped around and whacked Candayce's back.

"Okay, what do we do?" Janine said.

Janine picked up the egg she'd just saved. The other Triceratops watched her carefully as she moved in front of McGurk. She waved her beak back and forth and acted as if she might drop the egg.

McGurk snorted. His head lowered. His twisting horns came level with Janine.

Around her, other Triceratops gathered.

"Yum, yum, yum, McGurk! I'm hungry. Come on. I'm making you mad—*do something!*"

McGurk flung himself forward. Janine darted back, tripped, and the egg fell from her beak. Janine fell on her rump, her wings outstretched, and nearly howled with laughter as she saw McGurk hauling Candayce away from the collapsing pit.

And he kept coming!

"Oh, no," Janine whispered. She got to her feet, spread her wings, and sensed—a thermal. The current was low. She caught the breeze and was whipped into the air above the heads of the other Triceratops. She spun, spiraled, danced, felt the freedom she thought lost to her forever, and fell in a heap.

Thundering footsteps chased after her. She saw McGurk heading her way, along with his buddies.

"*STOP!*"

Candayce's command rang in her mind. It was the

most grating, wretched, and insanely beautiful thing she'd ever heard, and it made the Triceratops halt their gallop.

"Enough already," Candayce said.

The Triceratops agreed. As they went back to their young, Candayce walked over to Janine.

"I'm starved," she said. "Let's get something to eat, then get some rest."

"Sounds good," Janine said.

CHAPTER 10

CANDAYCE

Candayce and Janine had spent the day sprinting along riverbanks, then following a trail only Candayce could see. Janine, worried about being lost despite Candayce's almost mystical certainty, scratched her tag into every fourth tree.

Twilight was upon them, and Janine was still nursing her wounded arm, though she'd complained about it less as the day wore on.

Candayce had the feeling Janine had dislocated a bone, then wrenched it back into place during the climb to save the eggs. But she wasn't going to say anything, because it might lead to yelling and screaming, and when they were just talking, it was surprisingly nice.

Ahead stretched plains interrupted by rocks, moss, shrubs, fallen trees, and wide, snaking cracks in the earth. Tall shapes loomed on the horizon—perhaps the area where she'd left Mike and Bertram. But

Candayce couldn't get excited yet because they'd been *looming* in the same position for a very long time.

"You think *Keith* is good-looking?" Janine asked, amazed.

"Don't you?"

"I think he's stuck-up."

"The two don't exactly cancel each other out." Candayce shook her head. "Look, 'eighth-grade studs' isn't a safe topic. Why don't we move—"

"Keith is not a stud."

"Fine."

"Mike, maybe, not Keith."

Candayce whirled on Janine.

"You're right, let's change the subject," Janine said.

Candayce suggested a game she liked to play with her folks on long trips. "The whole thing is, I'm seeing something, and you have to figure out what I'm seeing."

"Yeah, all right."

Candayce spotted something in the distance. "I spy with my little eye something beginning with the letter *I*." A bug whapped Janine's beak. She ate it.

"You're disgusting."

"At least I don't drag vines around and floss with them—"

"Maybe you should!"

Janine's shoulders sagged. "The letter *I*?"

"I don't know if I'm speaking to you."

"Of course you are. You'd go insane if you couldn't hear the sound of your own voice."

"Still wouldn't need you for that."

"Yes, you do, you have to have an audience—"

"*The letter* I!" Candayce wailed.

Janine looked around. "Insects?"

"Yeah..."

Candayce said, "I spy with my little eye—what *is* that thing?"

An eleven-foot-long dinosaur plodded across the plain. It looked like a cross between an egg-stealer and an iguana, with a glimmering jade body and rows of bony studs along its back. It kept looking over its shoulder at a tall outcropping of rock.

"Doesn't count if neither of us knows what it is."

Candayce shook her head. A few pale stars appeared overhead. "We should find someplace to dig in for the night."

Janine stopped suddenly. "Over there."

"What?"

"I spy, with my little eye, something beginning with—"

"*Mike!*" Candayce exclaimed.

Ahead, a T. rex and an Ankylosaurus came around a large boulder. Candayce dropped to all fours and galloped their way. "*Mike! Bertram!*"

They were out and they were all right, and before Candayce knew exactly what she was doing, she ran up to Bertram and *kissed him!*

For an instant, all of the Cretaceous fell away. Even though Candayce knew she was kissing the rough equivalent of a horned rhino, even though she couldn't even feel that much, it was all right, because Bertram, that great gaseous windbag, smelled and tasted like—

Peppermint. Candayce drew back.

"I found these tiny little plants along the ground," Bertram said. "I know this is the age of the flowering plants and flowering herbs, but, boy, they tasted good, and it's kind of like mouthwash, and...Hi."

Janine caught up with Candayce. "How?"

Mike came around Bertram. "The second quake. It filled in the corridor where we'd started. It made shelves. It was tough going, but we climbed out."

"Moriarty was there," Bertram said.

Mike laughed. "Yeah. Bertram kicked his butt."

"Bertram?" Candayce asked.

"Look at him. He's a tank."

Candayce nodded. She felt her eyes beginning to tear. She opened her arms and pressed herself between Mike and Bertram, awkwardly managing to hug them both as she started to sob.

A sharp cry from above startled her. Candayce looked up to see a Quetzalcoatlus soaring above.

"Loki," Janine whispered.

Candayce was stunned. She'd been wrong, and about the one thing she was certain she knew above all others—guys. Yet here Loki was. "I guess I don't know everything."

Janine nodded. "I guess neither of us does."

Candayce watched as Janine ran after him. She spread her wings, flapped a few times, and leaped into the air. She didn't fly long. She didn't fly fast. But she flew. And for some reason, the sight couldn't have made Candayce happier.

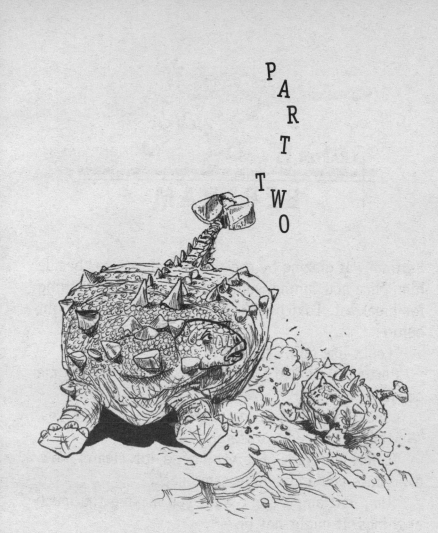

PART
TWO

Ankylosaurus
Ambush

CHAPTER 11

BERTRAM

Bertram was grazing by the river. Candayce was beside him. Mike and Janine were at the river's edge, fishing for breakfast. Loki hadn't been seen since the night before.

"Looks like rain," Candayce said.

Bertram shrugged. "I'm not gonna let that get me down."

Candayce nibbled on some peppermint leaves. "Bertram, you seem...different."

"I *feel* different. Everything's a lot clearer now, ever since you and Janine came back."

"Um, Bertram, I don't want you making too much of things. It might not be—"

"You're worried about that kiss you gave me."

Candayce's beak opened wide. "Yeah."

"Don't. It wasn't that great."

"Excuse me?"

"It woke me up to a lot of things. I mean, I know what I *thought* it was going to be like, but...it was actually like being kissed by my sister."

"Your sister! You don't even *have* a sister."

Bertram chomped on the smorgasbord of leaves. "It's wonderful. I'm *cured*. One minute all I could think about was you, the next I can't believe I was acting so dopey."

Candayce's shoulders hunched. "Can we drop this?"

"Sure, I—"

"Thank you."

Despite the clouds and the storm that was already hitting hard in the distance, Bertram felt wonderful. He had a sense that today would be special. A day that would change his life forever. A song came into his head, and he wiggled his backside, dancing and singing along with the beat.

"Who taught you how to dance?" Candayce asked.

Bertram looked over at Candayce. "No one."

"I can tell. Come on, crank it up again."

Bertram did. Candayce cried, "Now watch me!" She bumped her hips, rolled her shoulders, slapped her tail, and started bouncing around from claw to claw. Bertram's head bobbed in time with the beat. He kicked up one foot, planted it. Kicked up the other, planted it. Then his head whipped around.

"You got it goin' on!" Candayce said, dancing as the music swelled.

For the first time in his young life, Bertram believed it!

CHAPTER 12

MIKE

"Do you believe you're seeing this?" Janine asked.

Mike laughed. Candayce and Bertram were rocking out on the shore, dancing and wiggling and thumping and giggling. Unreal. "It *is* great, though," Mike said.

"Yeah..."

"Wanna dance?" Mike started swishing his tail, rolling his shoulders, waving his little arms.

Janine looked at the storm clouds nervously. "Nah. I don't like the look of things."

"Right." Mike plunged his muzzle into the water and came up with a mouthful of fish. Beside him, Janine snagged a few herself. Three-foot-long turtles drifted by. An enormous five-and-a-half-foot flounder with gold plating bumped into Mike's leg.

They stepped out of the water. Janine swallowed her meal, then studied the heavens. Mike felt a little nervous. It had been a day of hard travel after Janine came back, and she'd said little about why she'd left them in the first place. No one had asked her about it, either. It was as if they were afraid of the answer.

"Bertram's got your key chain," Mike blurted. "It's wrapped around a couple of his spikes. Kept meaning to mention it to you."

"That's okay. Thanks."

She didn't say whether she would bother retrieving it. Mike wished he knew what was on her mind.

"I'm curious," Janine said suddenly. "Remember the first time we went fishing? I could see something was bothering you."

Mike nodded slowly.

"It was something to do with back home, right?"

Mike considered the situation. He was suddenly anxious to talk about it. "Janine, I—"

"I mean, here you are, Mike Peterefsky. You've got what anyone who isn't you would consider a perfect life, and that world back there was crushing you just like it was crushing all the rest of us. That's the truth, isn't it?"

"Yeah. But some of it I brought on myself. See, there's this thing that Sean—"

"I don't want the gory details," Janine said. "I just want to know if I was right."

"You were right. But that doesn't mean things can't change. Look at us. We're changing history."

"Are we?"

"Mr. London said if we were hearing his message, then we'd already made sure that his future would never come to pass."

"Oh, yeah? If that future never happens, how could he have sent the message?"

Mike froze at the thought. "I don't—"

Janine shook her head. "Forget it. I woke up feeling really negative."

Mike surveyed the horizon nervously.

"Don't lose sleep over what I just said. I'm sure there's some time paradox or something. Maybe sixty years after we get back, Bertram will be sitting there with Mr. London, telling him what message to send. Anything's possible."

"Yeah," Mike said distractedly.

"You're not worried about what I said, are you? You're thinking about Moriarty."

"That obvious, huh?"

"Yep."

"I know what Coach Garibaldi would say. It's mind over matter. If you don't mind, it don't matter." Mike laughed.

A cloudburst overhead made him jump, and a cold, biting rain beat down upon them. "We'd better find somewhere to wait this out."

Janine was silent, staring at the river.

"What's the matter?"

Strangled cries escaped her. Mike saw a curtain of brown mist a few hundred yards downriver, moving their way. In seconds, it swallowed the horizon.

Then there was no more time for thought. The wall was upon them, and the mist he'd seen was little more than a herald of the all-encompassing flood of rain and rising water that snapped trees and swallowed anything in its path.

Like them.

CHAPTER 13

CANDAYCE

"Flash flood!" Bertram raced for the trees.

Candayce couldn't move. There was nowhere to go, and she knew it.

"Bertram! What do we do?"

The Ankylosaurus was falling over his own feet. He'd suddenly forgotten how to be a dinosaur and was trying to run like a thirteen-year-old human.

"Bertram!" Candayce screamed. "What do we do?"

The club-tail looked at her, eyes wide.

She'd considered talking with Bertram about how far behind they'd gotten, how little chance they had of finding the Standing Stones in time, and if anyone besides Janine had actually considered what life would be like if they were trapped forever in this era. The prospect of a future in the Late Cretaceous certainly hadn't thrilled her. But staring at the rushing wall of mud, she concluded that any future was better than no future at all.

"We need you, Bertram! Tell us what to do!"

Then the tough resolve he'd displayed returned. "Don't fight it. Let it carry you! Don't panic!"

The water slammed into Candayce. She was blinded and gagged by the foul-smelling mud and water. She sank, panic taking hold.

The river grasped her, and she felt things knocking into her. Rocks. Tree trunks. Fish. She prayed as the flood carried her along.

Then she burst to the surface, gasping for air. She looked around for the others as the river swept her on, but all she could see were blurs.

Thunder bellowed, competing with the roar of the river. She was dragged farther and farther, her thoughts on the world she was certain she'd lost, and on Bertram, Mike, and even Janine.

A swarm of ratlike mammals chittered around her, their furry bodies battering her skull before they were swept away by the waters. They were all at the mercy of the flood.

Candayce had never felt so small, so helpless.

She nearly fainted, but the water was cold and bracing. And as the flood whipped her about, Candayce realized that she was in a raging battle.

She was floating, twisting, her eyes squeezed shut, and suddenly, the rain stopped. Warmth seeped into her, and she opened her eyes.

The sun had come out. She was floating in the

shallows of the river, in a place she'd seen before. Or had she? Jagged white mountain peaks rose in the distance. Towering 130-foot spruce trees lined the shore. Odd slabs of stone thrust out of the water and stabbed into the shore like questing swords.

She was home. This was the Montana she knew!

She looked down at her claws. No. This only *looked* like home. Where was she? Where was everyone else?

Shattered trees floated around her as she swam for shore. She climbed out, her entire body vibrating as if the current had snaked its way inside her. Her ears popped, and she heard the steady hiss of the river. A dinosaur roared.

"Mike?" she called. "Bertram?"

No reply. In the forest, she found leaves and berries and ate greedily. Then she settled back and lay in a patch of golden sunlight, soaking up its heat.

She was alone. Mike and Bertram and Janine either hadn't made it through the flood, or they'd been deposited somewhere else along the countless miles of the river's length. If she met up with them, great. But the chances weren't good.

The roar came again. Closer this time. Candayce bolted to her feet.

The roar gave way to a sad cry. An invisible hand closed on Candayce's heart, tugging at it, and she wondered what was making that sound and why.

Leave it alone. Curiosity is not a good thing in the Late Cretaceous. You have to be tough. You're a dinosaur, got it? *Just an average, everyday—*

"Hah," Candayce muttered. "I've never been *average* in my life.*"* She didn't care what her inner dino was urging her to do, she was going to see what was making the noise. Maybe she could help. She carefully navigated the woods, and suddenly, a familiar stink came to her. "Bertram?"

Only the moaning answered her.

Candayce broke into a gallop, smashing branches, ignoring the rat-thingies and roaches and all the wretched little creatures of the forest in her blind, panicked flight. She yelled, *"Bertram!"*

The gas scent was overpowering. Disgusting. But right now, that smell was as welcome as a whiff of Chanel. It was Bertram. It had to be!

Candayce burst through the trees onto a lush plain. A jagged tributary of the river cut through the green, and a club-tail stood at the edge of the water.

"Bertram!" Candayce raced to the club-tail, thinking, *So my kiss didn't do anything for you, huh? Just wait until you get this one, you big, fat, adorable—*

The club-tail turned in Candayce's direction.

She stopped close enough to know she'd made a mistake. The Ankylosaurus, eyes burning with rage, roared and raised its tail again. It advanced on Candayce.

Two things were now fearfully obvious: This club-tail wasn't Bertram—and she was in trouble.

CHAPTER 14

BERTRAM

Bertram had known that Triceratops and other large dinosaurs had the ability to swim. It made sense to him that an Ankylosaurus could do it, too.

He had clung to that hypothesis as the river carried him to his fate. He'd bounced around like the ball in a pinball game, he'd spun like a bottle cap, and he'd taken some bruises, but he'd *survived*.

After hours as a prisoner of the flood, Bertram climbed onto the riverbank and dropped to the ground, panting with relief. He knew this mountainous area, although not from his own time. Despite some superficial similarities, sixty-seven million years had wrought many changes in these lands—or would, to be more precise. No, he recognized this land from computer re-creations, from diagrams, from texts he'd studied. And if he was right, they were less than a day's journey from the Standing Stones!

They? Bertram looked around. "Mike? Candayce?"

No answer.

"Janine!"

Silence.

Bertram's greatest concern was for the fragile, hollow-boned Janine. The brutal trip downriver had been tough enough for him to endure. But for her...

Bertram looked over his shoulder and saw part of a tree trunk jammed onto his spikes. Janine's chain of shells was trapped beneath it. Many of the shells had been crushed, but a few remained.

He wiggled a little. *Cha-ching!* The noise gave him comfort—and hope. Now to find the others. It occurred to him that Mike had the best nose and therefore the greatest chance of reuniting them.

His best bet was to grab some food and let nature—via his digestive system—take its course. Then he would sit here, where he could easily be smelled—and eventually be found.

There was danger, naturally. Some predator might find him first. But he could handle himself.

Bertram found some low-lying shrubs and went to work. He thought of the event he'd just miraculously survived. Flash floods were the allies of paleontologists. They served to bury fallen tree trunks and all kinds of life beneath tons of sand and silt, creating the conditions necessary for fossilization.

Bertram's dad had described flash floods as nature doing a little remodeling. Often, entire mountains were robbed of several layers of soil, and the valleys through which the flood traveled resurfaced.

A familiar voice interrupted Bertram's thoughts. *"Get away from me, you horny witch!"*

Candayce!

"I'm coming," Bertram called. "I'm coming!"

He stomped off, following the steady stream of psychic cries and curses. To make a path for himself, he had to knock down baby Araucaria, or monkey-puzzle trees—spiny affairs that were only ten feet tall now but would have easily grown to one hundred. Soon, Candayce's yells stopped.

Bertram heard roars and deep, melancholy bellows. By the time he reached the verdant plain where Candayce had been facing her terrible trial—whatever it had been—all the excitement had faded. Candayce sat across from an Ankylosaurus. They stared at each other warily. Both seemed depressed.

"You know what I would give for a box of Cracker Jacks right now?" Candayce asked. "I would eat *cafeteria* food, and I would *like* it."

Bertram barely heard her. His attention was on the club-tail. *This* was what he looked like to others. It was a female. He could sense it. "Magnificent," he whispered.

The Ankylosaurus grunted inquisitively. Her eyes were dark and filled with an inexpressible longing. She took a step back to the water. "It's all right," Bertram said. "No one's going to hurt you."

Candayce nodded. "I know she's not going to hurt

me. I just spooked her, I guess."

"I wasn't talking to you."

Candayce dropped her parrotlike head on her dumpy chest and said, "Of course not."

The second Ankylosaurus stopped backing up. Bertram came a little closer, staring in wonder at the spiky two-ton tank.

Suddenly, a cry sounded from the other side of the creek. *"Bertram! Candayce!"*

Bertram saw Mike charging their way. The T. rex splashed into the creek, heedless of the danger. The female Ankylosaurus chuffed and backed up in pure terror.

"Mike, wait!" Bertram yelled to the ecstatic Tyrannosaurus. Mike was beyond listening. He tore through the creek, whooping and hollering.

Behind Bertram, the second Ankylosaurus raised her tail. She darted frantically as she surveyed the flatland. Bertram guessed she was looking for a better battlefield. Finding none, she was preparing to make her stand here.

"He's not going to hurt you," Bertram said.

Then Mike was upon them. Bertram raised his tail—and *whacked* Mike in the stomach!

Mike grunted, the wind driven out of him. He teetered, then fell backward. Candayce scrambled out of the way as he hit the ground, the impact spewing chunks of dirt and ferns everywhere.

The female Ankylosaurus hurried around Bertram,

her tail raised over Mike's skull. She was moving in for the kill.

"Wait! Stop!" Bertram screamed. He shoved himself against the newcomer just as her tail slammed down, missing Mike's head by inches.

"Hey!" Mike cried. "What is this?"

Mike was about to stand when Bertram's tail smashed once more into his belly. Back he went, crashing onto the ground, making the earth shake.

"I don't wanna wrestle!" Mike growled.

Before the female could make another move, Bertram put his tail against Mike's neck.

"Be submissive," Bertram commanded.

"This I gotta see," Candayce muttered.

Mike sighed and lay back, putting his claws in the air and showing his belly. "There. Is this enough?"

The female was staring at Bertram in awe. Her tail dropped all the way to the ground, and she averted her gaze.

"I'm taking that as a good sign." Bertram raised his tail. Mike got up slowly.

The female approached Bertram carefully, eyeing Mike the entire time. She nuzzled Bertram's neck and licked the side of his face. Embarrassed, Bertram looked toward Mike and Candayce.

"My hero," Candayce said flatly.

Mike nudged her. "Shh."

From above, a shrill cry sounded. *Cahhhwr!*

Bertram looked up to see Janine circling above.

"You made it!"

"Mike saw the flood coming and grabbed me with his jaws and tossed me high," Janine called. "I got lucky and caught a current, then I rode out the flood in the air. My arm's pretty sore, but I'm okay."

She came in for a graceful landing.

"Wow," Bertram said. Beside him, the female Ankylosaurus tapped her tail against his. Bertram took a few steps, and she scrambled after him. She stared right at him, plaintively. When he looked away, she raced around so that he could see her face.

BRRAHHPPTT!

Bertram shuddered as his digestive process kicked in. "Sorry."

The female nuzzled him again. Everyone else backed away until the wind carried off the worst of the fumes. Bertram looked over to see the female staring in fear and distrust at Mike.

"Mike, could you come here?" Bertram asked.

"I don't want to scare your friend."

"Come here. Please."

Mike wandered over. The female bared her teeth and swiped her tail from side to side.

"You're not gonna hit me again?" Mike asked.

"See this log on my back?" Bertram said. "Could you get it off for me?"

Using his tail, Bertram nudged the female away. She cried out, but Bertram stamped his feet.

"Bertram—"

"Consider it a show of faith. She needs to know you're not dangerous. Besides, it's itching."

Mike nodded. He opened his maw and bit into the log. He yanked it off Bertram's spikes and tossed it into the creek. Then he backed away.

The female looked at Bertram as if he was a god.

"Show-off," Candayce said. "I tamed the mighty T. rex, *baby*. Wanna take a spin?"

"It's not like that," Bertram said. Though, in his heart, he wasn't entirely sure. "Oh, Janine! Your chain, it's still on my spikes—"

"I've kinda gotten used to not having it," Janine said. "Why don't you keep it for now?"

Bertram nodded. He didn't like the sound of that, but he wasn't going to start something he wasn't prepared to finish. They needed Janine.

"I have some news," Bertram said. "We're about twenty-five miles from the Standing Stones. We're going home!"

Mike, Candayce, and Janine were silent. Then Candayce started to cry, and Mike held her as best he could. Janine stalked to Bertram and plucked her chain from his spikes. She walked off, whipping it hard. *Cha-ching!*

"I don't get it," Bertram said. "I thought everyone would be happy."

"We are," Mike said, brushing his snout over the top of Candayce's scaly head. "We are."

Bertram looked at the female. She was wandering

away, but still glanced his way, as if she wanted him to follow. He wasn't sure why, but he did. "I'll be back. Wait there." Bertram followed the female through twisting woods—Araucaria and Picea, thirteen-story-high spruce—then back to the riverbank.

They walked together until they came to what looked like a boulder half stuck in the sand, silt, and shimmering water. It took Bertram a moment to understand that he was looking at the body of another Ankylosaurus. A male.

He looked at the female. "Your mate."

The mournful sound he'd heard before issued from her lips. Then she nuzzled Bertram.

"Don't worry," he said. "I won't abandon you. I mean, not right away. We'll find a place for you..."

Closing his eyes, he nuzzled the female back.

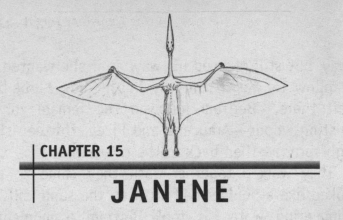

CHAPTER 15

JANINE

Janine soared over the cliffs as the last moments of daylight played upon the horizon. Bands of rich violet and pale blue had been painted across the sky by a hand infinitely more skilled than her own. The sun was a crimson sphere sinking beyond the end of the world.

She had to see the Standing Stones. Bertram had placed an image of them in her mind, but it wasn't enough. So she'd ignored the pain in her arm and flown off in search of them. She'd suffered flares of wrenching hurt as she'd flown, but she had to see, had to *know* if the way back was really there.

Studying the ground below, she saw that it wouldn't be long now. The plateau had to be dead ahead.

She flew, the plateau coming into sight. And at its apex stood—nothing at all.

Janine circled frantically. She studied the terrain, convinced she made an error. But there'd been no mistake. They'd all come so far for nothing.

Janine screamed in rage. She dived toward the ground as the last pale rays of sunlight faded. Her vision blurring, she came to an awkward landing on the plateau and collapsed.

It was too dark to find her way back now. Besides, she needed time to think.

What was she so upset about, anyway? She'd made the decision not to go back. She'd only accompanied the others to help *them* find this place. *They* were the ones who wanted to leave. *She* was the one who belonged here.

Janine thought about Candayce's revelations. *Mom knows,* Janine thought.

All the more reason to stay. She wouldn't ever have to worry about causing her mother grief again.

Besides, she didn't have any choice in the matter. Bertram had been wrong. Mr. London had been wrong. She'd trusted them, just as she'd trusted her dad to come home that summer, and they'd all let her down.

A *caw!* interrupted her thoughts. Janine looked up and saw Loki. He'd returned, as she knew he would. Right now, she wouldn't say no to his company.

Come first light, she'd fly down to her friends and tell them the bad news.

CHAPTER 16

BERTRAM

"PAHHHRRR-TEEE!" Mike howled.

Bertram watched as Mike and Candayce danced. Music flooded the pebble-strewn area they'd chosen for the night. They'd already shaved eight miles off their journey. By dinnertime tomorrow, they'd be home.

Behind Bertram there was a whimper. He looked back to see the female shuddering.

"The music's scaring her," Bertram told Candayce. "Keep it down!"

The tune only got louder.

"You got it! You got it!" Candayce yelped to Mike.

Bertram slammed his tail down with explosive force. Candayce was knocked over. Mike wobbled a little.

The music stopped.

"What's your *problem?*" Candayce snarled.

"Your *music* was frightening her. I asked nicely. Now knock it off!"

Mike sat back against a tree. "Oh, man, I can't wait

to get out on the field, throw a few passes." He lowered his head. "I wonder if it'll be the same day when we get back?"

"I have to feed the fish," Candayce said. "I forgot to do it before I left! I mean, before...y'know..."

"Yeah, and I have to do *everything*," Bertram said. The entire upkeep of his household, even paying the bills, was in his hands.

Candayce set her claws on her hips and walked over. "I understand what you're feeling. The same thing happened to me when I met up with other Leptoceratops. There's all this *stuff* that gets opened up inside you, and it's confusing. But the important thing—"

"Please," Bertram said. "This has nothing to do with Beanie."

"Beanie?"

"Well, she's...brown. And round. Like a bean."

"Beanie. Like...what I wore when I was a Brownie? When you used to follow me all over the place?"

"It's not like that."

Candayce rolled back. "Mike!"

"Um?"

"Bertram's got a girlfriend!"

"Do not!" Bertram kicked at Candayce.

"Studly!" Mike called.

"Isn't she *sweet?*" Candayce burbled in baby talk. "Are we going to take her to the prom?"

"Just shut up."

"You shut up," Candayce said. "I—hey!"

A huge club-tail nearly smashed Candayce into the ground. Bertram looked around in shock and saw Beanie advancing on Candayce.

"Call her off!" Candayce yelped. "Tell her I'm sorry!"

Beanie whacked the ground again, making Candayce barrel into Mike's stubby arms. Mike roared. It wasn't much of a roar, but it was enough to make Beanie quit. The female Ankylosaurus strutted over to Bertram. She settled down beside him and started licking his jowls.

"Very nice," Mike said.

"She's crazy!" Candayce hollered.

Bertram sank on his haunches. "She's *protective*. She lost her mate. He drowned in the river."

Candayce stepped away from Mike. "So she really has, like, adopted you?"

"I think it's more serious than that."

"You mean...she wants you to be her, uh..."

"Glad to know you find that a ridiculous notion."

"No, I—"

"From what I understand, she's grieving, and she doesn't want to be alone. I'm just worried about tomorrow. I don't know if she can handle another loss so soon."

Mike shook his head. "It's possible you're reading too much into things."

"Yeah," Candayce said. "I know when guys have gotten crushes on me—"

Beanie surged forward, her tail up and swinging.

"Yiiiiiee!" Candayce yipped, racing back to Mike. "Okay, fine! She wants you. You're the man!"

"You know," Mike said, "she might like the music if you were the one making it."

"Yeah, that's a good idea!" Candayce said. "Start with something light. Classical."

"I don't know much classical..."

"*1812 Overture*. Everyone knows that. They play it every July Fourth."

"I thought you said *light*."

"It starts soft, then builds up. It's perfect."

Bertram sighed and turned to Beanie. "Don't be afraid. This is music. It's something from my world."

He concentrated. *Nah-nah nah-nah nah-nah nah NAH...boom boom...*

"Grmph?" Beanie asked.

Bertram let the music rise up around them.

Nah-nah nah-nah nah-nah nah-nah nah NAH... boom—

BHHHRAPHHHPTTT!

"Whoa!" Bertram was enveloped by a noxious cloud. Beanie had eaten just an hour ago.

"Not again!" Candayce yelled.

"We're heading upwind!" Mike warned.

Bertram drew closer to Beanie. "That was on the beat," he said. "Did you do that on purpose?"

He started the music again, and this time, just when the cannons were about to fire—

BHHHRAPHHHPTTT!

She did it again! He kicked up the music, and the next time, *he* did it! Beanie started swaying with the music, and they settled into a loud, smelly duet of dueling vapors. Bertram laughed and laughed.

It was a night to remember.

CHAPTER 17

MIKE

Mike Peterefsky walked through the dimly lit hospital corridor. The place was deserted, except for a room at the end of the hall. A light blazed there, and people were sobbing.

Mike knew whose room it was.

"No!" Mike screamed. He woke trembling, his thick skin tingling. He saw that he was alone, lying across the trail they'd found. A shape was moving in the darkness. Mike felt an icy fear overtake him. "Moriarty?"

"I'm afraid not, my dear Holmes," Bertram said.

Mike relaxed. "I thought Candayce had first watch tonight."

"I couldn't sleep, so I took over. What's wrong? I heard you cry out."

"It's nothing." *Liar,* Mike chided himself.

Bertram ambled close. "Worried about tomorrow?"

"Yeah." *That much is true, anyway,* Mike thought.

109

Bertram nodded. "I've been going over every discussion I've ever had with Mr. London. The inter-connectedness of all things. The way matter cannot be created or destroyed, and therefore our bodies in the twentieth century are made of the same stuff as the dinosaurs...theories of Stanislav Grof and Jung. But I still have no idea how the M.I.N.D. Machine did what it did, or why."

"What's the difference, Bertram?" Mike shrugged. "I mean, it just worked, right?"

"There's a reason for everything, isn't there? That's what my dad always says."

Mike thought about that. "Bertram, can I tell you something? Something I never thought I'd tell any-one, but...you're smart."

"So are you."

"But you don't have a problem opening up about stuff. I've never been good at saying what's bothering me. I always tried to act like everything's cool. But now..."

"Tell me."

"You might not like what you hear."

Bertram shook his head. "There isn't anything you can say that's going to change the way I think of you. Whatever it is, just tell me."

Mike took a deep, shuddering breath. "Sean's planned a hit on one of our own guys. It was gonna happen at practice. The day we got sent here."

"Why?"

Mike rolled his shoulders. "'Cause Sean's crazy. He's come to believe that it doesn't matter how people feel about you, so long as you end up on top."

"Predators," Bertram murmured. "Boy, do I know the type. Win at all costs."

Mike nodded.

"How long have you known?"

"A while." Mike felt too ashamed to tell him any more than that. "I don't know what to *do*. I love football. The game's my whole life. If I tell on Sean, that's it for me. The whole team's with him."

"Why?"

"They think this guy Lowell's responsible for losing the first two games of the season. He's not as big or strong or fast as some of the others. But Lowell's a good guy. He gives everything he has, and Coach Garibaldi says if someone is willing to make the sacrifices it takes to get on the team, if he plays with heart, if he gives his all, then he stays on the team."

Bertram was silent for several moments. "You don't have any idea how people see you. What you mean to them."

"What?" Mike was totally baffled.

"There are things you haven't thought of. But it's not going to do any good hearing them from me. You have to figure this out yourself. You will. I know."

Bertram walked away, then stopped. "Thanks for telling me. I've never had anyone...thanks. I'm gonna wake Candayce, have her take watch. Big day tomorrow. We need our sleep."

Mike watched the Ankylosaurus as he ambled off.

And even though he still didn't have any answers, Mike felt better than he had in a long time.

CHAPTER 18

BERTRAM

Bertram woke to the sound of a T. rex pacing.

"So...which of us tells him?" whispered Mike.

"I will, if you want." Janine's voice.

A low growl, then, "I'm not sure how he's gonna take it. Maybe I should talk to him."

"Fine. *Someone's* got to."

The voices receded. Bertram opened his eyes and saw Mike and Janine a hundred yards off, still chatting and moving farther away. Beanie stood before him. Bertram suspected Mike and Janine were probably worried about how attached he was becoming to her.

Beanie nudged Bertram. He saw a huge pile of rich green leaves, including peppermint and three clusters of berries.

"Breakfast in bed," Candayce said. She sat about a dozen feet away.

"Did you?" asked Bertram.

Candayce nodded toward Beanie. "She did it. She

gave *me* a few twigs caked with muck. I think she's trying to tell me something."

"Maybe," Bertram said, happily munching on the breakfast that had been laid out for him. At home, he would've been the one preparing the grub. He could not remember the last time *anyone* cooked for him.

Bertram looked at Beanie. "Thank you." A comforting warmth rose from her. Bertram shifted his gaze to Candayce. "Go on. Say it."

"I think it's kind of nice, actually."

"Really?" Bertram was stunned.

"Yep."

So did he. The thundering footfalls of the pacing T. rex grew louder. There were only conifers and a few bushes around. No flowering plants, no forests, just a scattering of trees. Bertram saw Mike and Janine about five hundred feet down the trail.

"I'm going to talk with Mike and Janine," Bertram said to Beanie. "You wait here."

Bertram turned, and Candayce broke into hysterical laughter. "What?" Bertram demanded.

Candayce rolled on the ground. "Janine painted graffiti on your butt."

"What's it say?"

"Wide Load." She couldn't stop giggling. Beanie approached, tail raised.

"Hey!" Candayce yelped.

"It's all right," Bertram said. Beanie backed off.

"And she put red flowers on your tail. Like you

would on the back end of a truck!"

Bertram brought his tail around. It *was* funny, he had to admit. And Janine must have flown some distance to find the necessary materials. There were no flowers around here.

He wondered what had possessed Janine to do such a thing. Shrugging, he walked a few yards, Beanie following. He glared at her. "No. *You* wait *here*."

Candayce sighed. "It works better if you say 'dear' or 'my little love monkey' or something like that.

Makes it sound like more of a request than an order."

"'My little love monkey?'"

"I've heard 'em all. Pathetic, huh?"

Bertram nodded. He nuzzled Beanie. She trilled. "Wait here, okay...dear?"

He turned, and she followed. "So much for your advice," Bertram growled.

"Hey, all I've got to go on are eighth-grade boys. Besides, I just had to hear you say it. You *stud*."

Bertram shook his head. He approached Mike and Janine, with Beanie and Candayce right behind him. Mike appeared nervous, Janine resolved.

"Thanks for the redecorating," Bertram said.

Janine looked away. "Sorry. Couldn't resist."

"What are you talking about?" Mike asked.

Bertram turned so Mike could see the graffiti. Mike growled, "*Jeez*, Janine..."

"I couldn't help myself." Janine looked back to Bertram. "You're not mad, are you?"

"Well, I *am* concerned about temporal anomalies. If this Ankylosaurus' shell were to become fossilized, and the 'paint' you used left a raised surface, paleontologists could find this writing and freak."

"So I shouldn't tell you about all the stuff I've been scratching into rocks, huh?"

"You didn't!"

Janine looked around innocently.

Mike cleared his throat. "We need to talk."

Bertram was about to demand that Beanie go with

them and to make it clear he would accept no other course of action—when Janine leaped in.

"The Standing Stones aren't standing," she said.

"What?" Bertram asked.

"I found the plateau last night. There were no big rock formations all clustered together."

"Did you go to the right place?"

"Everything else checked out."

Bertram shuddered. "I have to see this for myself."

Mike lowered his head. "That's what we thought you'd say."

"You two have been talking about this?" Bertram asked.

"It's not a conspiracy," Janine said. "Don't get paranoid."

"Yeah, we didn't say anything to Candayce," the T. rex said.

"Thanks," Candayce sniped.

Janine stepped forward. "It's gonna be all right. I figured it out. You were right about most of it, but not *all* of it. There's got to be another plateau where the Standing Stones are. It probably has to do with all the earthquakes and shifting of land masses. There's no reason to panic. Mike and I can scout the area—"

Bertram slammed his tail on the ground. "I'm not wrong!"

"Bertram..." Mike said, studying his feet.

"I *know* it. I can *feel* it."

Janine spread her wings. "You made a mistake,

Bertram. You're human. Admit it and move on."

Candayce pointed at Janine. "Why should we listen to you? You don't *want* to go back."

"I—" Janine hung her head. "The *three* of you don't belong here. I want to help you get back."

"Sure," Candayce said. "But Bertram told us it's possible that either all four of us go back at the same time or none of us might make it through."

"I don't think that's true anymore," Bertram said.

"If I wanted to abandon the three of you, I could have done it!" Janine cried.

"Like before?" Candayce asked.

"Yes, like before. But I'm here, aren't I? Your *therapist* should have told you to judge people by what they do, not by what they say."

"Therapy?" Mike asked.

"Cheap shot." Candayce fixed her gaze on Janine. "I want to see this plateau."

"I've been there," Janine said. "There are no Standing Stones. What part can't you grasp?"

"Great," Mike said. "Now we're going to start fighting among ourselves."

Bertram stared at the T. rex. "You know you can trust me. I've gotten us this far."

"Actually, you haven't," Janine said. "It was fate. Dumb luck."

"Fate and luck aren't the same," Candayce said.

Janine shook her beak. "Whatever. Bertram didn't bring us here intentionally. It was a one-in-a-billion shot, an accident. He even said so."

The Ankylosaurus hung his head. "That's true."

"Don't you get it?" Janine asked. "Life is random. It doesn't go according to *anyone's* plan. I believed in this *map* Bertram had in his head because I didn't have anything else to believe in. Same goes for the message from Mr. London. But now—"

Mike growled. "We did it Bertram's way, and it didn't work out. Now we have to try something else."

"No," Candayce said. "I'm with Bertram. We stick to the plan. We go to the plateau."

Bertram did his best to conceal his surprise. His tail touched hers. "Thank you."

Janine shook her head. "Fine. Mike and I will start scouting."

Bertram exchanged a panicked glance with Candayce.

"Wait!" Candayce cried.

They stopped.

"Janine—give me your chain."

"What?"

"You can't trust in anything, can you?" Candayce asked. "You don't have it in you."

Janine unhooked her chain and handed it to Candayce.

Candayce whipped the chain out. *Cha-ching!* "Okay, here's the deal. You say everything's chance, right?"

Janine nodded.

"So let's make it a coin toss. If the shell you

scratched *good-bye* into comes up heads, you guys win. I'll go with Bertram to the plateau, and you two can meet us there later. Tails, we go together."

"Candayce—" Bertram didn't like this.

"Hey, come on. It's a fifty-fifty shot."

"Do it." Janine said.

Candayce hurled the chain into the air. Bertram tensed as he watched it flip and dance in the sunlight. Then it came crashing to the ground, scarred side up. Bertram hung his head in defeat.

"That proved nothing," Janine said, snatching her chain from the ground.

"Wait," Mike said. "Maybe they've got a point."

Janine stared. "We made a deal—"

"It can't be random," Mike said. "There's got to be a reason for this."

"I don't believe it." Janine shook out her wings.

"Bertram didn't make the M.I.N.D. Machine thinking it could send us back in time," Mike said. "But I have to believe that some part of him had an idea of where we were heading and that we needed a chance to think about what we were doing with our lives."

"Mike—" Janine said impatiently.

"Every time I've trusted Bertram, everything's come out okay. I think I need to believe that one more time."

"Do you think we'll walk into that valley and the Standing Stones are just going to magically appear?" Janine asked.

"Mr. London *did* say there was one last thing we had to know, something we had to do," Bertram said. "Maybe it's going to the Standing Stones together, whether all four of us decide to come back or not. Maybe that's what it'll take to open the doorway."

"The rocks aren't going to materialize!" Janine cried.

"Maybe they will," Mike said. "We're sixty-seven million years in the past. We've survived fire, flood, and earthquakes. We've taken everything this world can throw at us, and we're still here. If that's possible, then I don't see what's so strange about a couple of rocks popping out of nowhere."

"Mike—" Janine said desperately.

"We go to the plateau. If there's nothing there, we'll scout the area. All right?"

"If that's how you want it."

"It is," Mike said.

"Thank you," Bertram said. He could feel deep within him that this last opportunity was all he needed. For an instant, he felt like whooping and dancing—then he looked to Beanie. He nuzzled her and the group set out together.

CHAPTER 19

MIKE

"You'll never guess what I just found!" Janine squawked from overhead.

Mike looked up. They'd been climbing for five hours, and he was beginning to feel irritable. "What?"

"Nothing! I've been to the plateau again. There are *still* no rocks!"

"Just the ones in your head," Candayce muttered.

Janine fluttered her wings. "Funny. Can't you do better than that?"

"You're not worth 'better' today."

"How much longer?" Mike called.

"You're pretty close. About twenty minutes."

"You said that an hour ago!" Candayce yelled.

"Well, you're *slow*."

Mike drew in a deep breath of cool, crisp mountain air. They had walked a good five miles to a range of mountains. Janine had led them to a solitary peak with a winding path around its lower reaches.

The trail had been treacherous. Mike went first,

clearing trees and rocks to make the journey easier for Bertram and Beanie.

About a hundred feet up, the ledge had spilled down toward the waiting abyss. Mike couldn't see how the two Ankylosaurus would manage falling off the mountain. But Bertram had come up with the idea of stomping footholds and using his tail for balance. Beanie had mimicked his moves, and they had pulled through.

Now they were close. Above, Janine cawed. "I'm going to find a snack. Back soon!"

Mike watched as she flew off, haunted by her words. *The three of you don't belong here.* Meaning that she did. And looking at her graceful form soaring, he wondered if she was right.

"It's odd," Bertram said. "This trail looks perfectly natural, but I have a strange feeling about it."

"Like what?" Mike asked.

"It's been well traveled, possibly by dinos as large as we are. That's why it's so smooth."

Mike looked for tracks. He saw some small ones, but he had no idea what had made them. They weren't Moriarty's tracks.

He looked at the hard ground behind him. *He'd* barely left any tracks. Moriarty *could* already be ahead of them. Lying in wait. Preparing a trap.

Janine would have seen him. *Unless he's hiding.*

"Mike?" Bertram asked.

He turned to face darkness. It was a cave! A few rocks tumbled out and struck Mike's feet. There was a skittering, scratching, scraping sound. Mike's heart thundered. Moriarty could be hiding in the cave!

Mike tensed as he saw something approaching from the mouth of the cave. Eyes...claws...

"Ook!" it cried.

Two more shadows ran beyond it. "Eek!" "Ack!"

Suddenly, a trio of shapes burst from the darkness. Three dinosaurs, each fifteen feet long and seven feet tall. They had thick dome-shaped heads and purple, brown, and white scales. They crowded the path.

"Pachycephalosaurus!" Bertram cried. "Bone-headed dinos! I'd hoped to see some Pachys!"

"Great," Mike said. "Glad you're excited."

"Ookeekack!" one of the Pachys cried. He put his head down and rammed Mike's leg! Mike teetered and nearly fell. Bending, he opened his maw wide and snatched up the offending bonehead. He tossed the Pachy at his pals. They scrambled back into the darkness.

"Ookeekack! Ookeekack!"

Bertram shook his head. "Well, at least now we know what to call them."

They walked on, hearing occasional peeps from the Pachys.

"I wonder what that was all about?" Mike asked.

"I suppose they're territorial," Bertram said.

"They might have had young," Candayce noted.

Mike shrugged. "I guess we'll never know."

They were halfway around the mountain when a sudden vibration came from beyond a sharp turn.

Mike suddenly wished Janine hadn't flown off.

"Oh, no," Candayce said.

"What is it?" Mike asked.

Candayce's eyes widened. "Stampede!"

The thunder grew louder.

Bertram yelled, "Mike! Candayce! Get behind me!"

"What?" Mike asked.

"Do it! Quick!"

Mike felt like a coward, but he shuffled back anyway, grabbing the wall as he slid past Bertram on the narrow cliffside, Candayce ahead of him. "Bertram, tell me you know what you're doing."

Bertram's club-tail carved a defiant arc. "Batting practice."

Mike saw Beanie backing away from him in terror, her tail raised. Candayce touched Mike's hide. "If she thinks you're threatening Bertram, she's gonna charge—and I'm in between you!"

"It'll be all right."

"Oh, yeah. My brave strong man."

Mike saw Bertram moving to a wide spot on the ledge, near another cave. He brought his tail up and shifted his body to the side. *What if it's Moriarty?* Mike thought. *Bertram couldn't—*

Then a blur of shapes came racing around the corner. Pachys! Dozens of them, heads down like battering rams, in rows of four, like soldiers in a regiment.

"I don't suppose you'd stop if I asked you nicely," Bertram said.

The Pachys thundered on. Bertram waited until the Pachys were almost on him, then swung his tail. Pachys went flying to the left, piling up at the cave's mouth, or to the right, down the side of the mountain! Bertram's tail struck with a high, sharp *clack*. Mike could tell he was doing his best not to hurt the Pachys. He looked over the edge and saw boneheads scrambling to their feet.

Bertram whipped and struck until the way was clear. "All right, so it was more like bowling. I want to see this plateau."

Candayce kissed Bertram. "You did it!"

Beanie *grompf*ed angrily.

Candayce returned to Beanie. "Life is nasty, brutal, and short. Ask anyone who's ever been to gym class. Get over it!"

Beanie didn't get over it. She stalked forward.

Candayce let Beanie take her place behind Bertram. "Far be it from me to stand in the way of true love."

Mike led them forward. The addled Pachys near the cave's mouth looked at the group with wobbling heads and dark eyes.

"What was their problem?" asked Mike.

"No idea," Bertram said.

"Hey, Bertram!" Candayce called. "How about it?

Did *that* kiss do anything for you?"

Bertram was silent for a while.

"Skip it," Candayce said.

"You could try kissing me," Mike said.

"You've got fish breath. *He* tastes like peppermint."

They traveled unchallenged until a trio of Pachys appeared behind them.

"Ookeekack!"

"I wonder why they're acting this way?" Mike said. "Janine would have seen if there were nests or something like that on the plateau."

"Not necessarily," Bertram said. "There's a lot she could have missed."

Like the Standing Stones? Mike wanted so much to share in Bertram's vision, yet...

Mike noticed that Bertram had an odd look. "Something the matter?" he asked.

"All that talk about things happening for a reason made me think of an experiment Mr. London told me about. Quantum physicists divided a subatomic particle. The halves were separated by miles. When a clockwise spin was put on one half, its mate, miles away, began to spin at the exact same instant, at the exact same rate, in the exact same way.

"Scientists think this indicates that there really *is* some underlying force that connects all things. A pattern that gives form and structure to reality. These same particles are in all of us, in everything that was or ever will be. And they're connected to this pattern.

"Luck, coincidence, instinct, intuition—even what we feel for one another—all could be our minds establishing contact with this unifying pattern. If the M.I.N.D. Machine made contact with that pattern—well, it could explain a lot."

"How does that help us?" Mike asked.

Bertram shook his head. "If I'm right, a lot depends on how badly we *want* to go back."

Candayce laughed. "My bags are packed. I'm ready!"

Bertram wished it was that simple for him.

The trail rose higher and higher. They were almost there. Janine had said that the outer edge of the plateau rose up like the rim of a bowl.

Bertram was the first to see into the valley. He stopped. "Wow..."

"What is it?" Mike asked excitedly. "Can you see them?"

The club-tail didn't respond. Mike charged behind him, and Beanie cracked her tail down on the ledge menacingly. Bertram led Beanie onto the plateau. Mike saw them scramble through an opening to their left, then slide down and out of view. He looked to Candayce. "You go first. I'll keep an eye on the Pachys."

Candayce gasped when she saw the plateau.

Mike looked at the Pachys, who said, "Ook?"

"Sure," Mike replied. He went forward, his thoughts

weighed down with the possibilities. He turned to face the plateau. There were no Standing Stones. Janine had been right.

But something else was there: bones. The plateau was the equivalent of an elephant graveyard, with huge ribs and skulls half buried in the soft earth. At the far end of the plateau, up against a knife-sharp rise that went up a good hundred feet, he saw— movement. Mike moved to stand near Bertram and Candayce. Beanie looked around fearfully.

"Maybe it's the bones," Bertram sputtered.

Candayce sat down hard. "They're not here..."

Bertram began to pace. "Maybe, over time, the bones somehow become the Standing Stones. Or maybe the Standing Stones are really insect mounds that haven't yet been erected. Mr. London meant the *locale* where the Standing Stones would be, he—"

"But there is something..." Mike said.

He sniffed the air, but the stinky gas released by Bertram and Beanie had dulled his senses.

"In the shadows," Candayce said. "More Pachys."

"I don't know if we should stay here," Mike said. "It's a long walk down, and with the Pachys..."

"We need Janine!" Bertram cried. "All four of us have to be here—"

A sharp *caw* sounded, and Janine sailed over the group.

"Oh," she said. "Didn't see the bones. How could I have missed that?"

Bertram looked around desperately—but nothing happened. Janine was with them, but no miracles were taking place. The club-tail looked up and half sobbed, half shrieked, "All right! You win. It's not here. It's hopeless, all right? There, are you satisfied?"

Janine flew toward them, her wings opening wide. "Bertram, I'm sorry, I didn't want to hurt you."

Janine's foot touched the ground, and suddenly, a *shape* shimmered into existence before them. Everyone gasped.

"No," Mike said. "No way."

Facing Mike was an image he'd seen before: Hovering above the ground was a black metal slab. A *monolith.* The theme from *2001* came to Mike's mind.

"Wait," Bertram said, walking around the floating object. "We're seeing it from the side. From its edge."

Mike followed Bertram around the floating slab, and something else came into view.

"The M.I.N.D. Machine!" Bertram howled. "Look, it's the M.I.N.D. Machine!"

Mike heard something. Bones crunching underfoot. He felt vibrations. Heard ragged breathing.

"We're going *home!*" Candayce screamed.

"Yes! Yes!" Janine howled.

Bertram cried with happiness. "We needed to be *standing,* all four of us, standing here—"

Mike saw something behind the monolith. A huge, three-toed claw. A tail.

"No..."

Then a massive shape came out from behind the M.I.N.D. Machine. A twenty-foot T. rex that had been waiting for them. It was crazed, its eyes ablaze in the fiery sunlight.

"No," Mike whispered. "Please..."

It was Moriarty, and he was charging straight for Janine.

CHAPTER 20

MIKE

Mike froze as Moriarty plucked Janine up in his gaping maw. He held her by one twisted wing, his teeth resting almost tenderly upon her gullet.

"Mike!" she cried. "Mike, please help..."

Beanie pounded the ground with her tail, but Bertram hissed at her. Beanie drew back in confusion.

Mike stared into Moriarty's reddish eyes. "Let her go *now*."

Moriarty took a thundering step back.

"Oh, no, I'm gonna die," Janine whimpered.

Mike stepped forward. "Janine, you're not gonna die. You're not the one he wants."

Janine looked at the six-inch teeth holding her. "Oh? You sure about that?"

"Let...her...*go!*" Mike cried, as if he could command the giant rex with his will. Moriarty whipped Janine back and forth. She screamed—then sagged in his grasp. Mike yelled, *"Janine!"*

"She's all right," Bertram said. "Probably just the shock."

The giant rex stepped back again. And again.

"Why don't you leave us alone?" Mike cried.

"I don't think he can," Bertram said softly. "I think you've been drawing him here."

Mike couldn't believe he was hearing this. "You think I *want* him here?"

"No," Bertram said. "I don't think it's that simple."

Mike recalled Moriarty's ambush after the earthquake. The name he'd called the giant rex—

Sean, he thought feverishly, *Sean.*

Moriarty stepped back. Mike followed. It was like a frightening dance, with a horrifying price to pay for stepping on your partner's toes.

Mike stalked after Moriarty. With a muffled roar, the giant rex turned and loped off, toward the mountain. Mike charged after him.

"Mike, don't!" Bertram yelled.

It was a trap. It had to be.

Stop thinking of him as a person! Mike demanded. *He's not!*

The darkness swallowed Moriarty. Mike launched himself at his enemy—and struck a wall.

He heard Moriarty's growl. Above him, this time. Mike saw what looked like steps, spaced four or five feet apart, leading up and around to the back of the mountain.

Mike leaped toward the first step, then hopped to the next, and the next. He circled as he climbed. The ground was now far below. He felt rocks trickling down onto his head. Looking up, he saw Moriarty climbing a new trail along the rear of the mountain, Janine still cradled in his jaws.

Why doesn't he just eat her? Mike wondered. *Why's he keeping her alive?*

Memories of Moriarty flew into his brain. The way he hobbled the turtles so they couldn't get away, going after far more than he could possibly eat. And he thought of Sean, who was no longer happy with tackling an opponent and bringing him down. He'd calculated blows to take them out. Even if that "opponent" was one of their own, like Lowell.

Mike raced after the rex. He leaped and ran faster than he ever had before. He felt as if he was at a football game, only this time there was much more at stake than winning a game.

Janine—his friend.

The giant rex was above him now, slowing down. The apex of the mountain rose into view, and Mike saw two tall forms ahead as his ascent leveled out. A pair of boulders, like the upraised ends of a football goalpost, flanked a narrow trail. And—

He stopped, chest heaving, and waited.

Between the stones, he saw a shadow darting furtively on the ground.

Mike felt charged with the sudden, overwhelming

power of understanding. Moriarty had wanted Mike to run blindly between those posts. It *was* a trap. Moriarty had been playing him, just the way Sean had been playing him.

Like Moriarty, Sean had to prove that he was the superior predator. That he ruled without question.

Mike had challenged Moriarty's rule. Now the giant rex was using Janine as bait to draw him to his fall, just as Sean planned to use...

"Lowell," Mike whispered, seeing it clearly now. "Sean's *'Big Event'* was a trap. Only it wasn't just for Lowell. It was for the whole team. Especially for *me*."

A growl came from behind one of the goalpost stones. Mike studied the ground ahead. He saw a crumbling, six-foot shelf of earth, then *nothing*.

Very slowly, he walked between the upright stones. Moriarty was there. Janine was still in his maw.

"I'm here," Mike said. "Put Janine down, and we'll settle this."

Moriarty took a lurching step forward. Mike could feel the fragile layer of rock beneath them quiver. Moriarty's head lowered. He locked his gaze on Mike.

"Come on," Mike said. "You want to tear me up. That's good, 'cause I want you, too. But you can't fight with *that* in your mouth. Get rid of her."

Moriarty's shoulders hunched. He roared, opening his maw wide. Janine nearly toppled out, then Moriarty clamped down on her. He could have bitten her in half—but something stopped him.

"Mike...?" Janine whimpered.

Mike's nostrils flared. "Come on! Let her go. Let's finish it the way it was meant to be."

A strange light came into Moriarty's eyes. He looked down at the Quetzalcoatlus in his mouth and tossed her away.

Mike watched as Janine's crumpled form hit the rim of the ledge, bounced, then fell into the abyss.

"*No!*" Mike screamed. Only silence greeted him.

Moriarty roared—and Mike threw himself at the rex. They bit and growled and grunted, pain and fury mixing together, the human part of Mike's brain became one with the rex inside him, and he fought with all his heart.

Then Moriarty was sinking back. Mike drew away, his shoulder feeling like an exposed wound. He saw that Moriarty looked even worse.

"Let it go," Mike said. "It can end here and now."

Moriarty's response was to lurch upward, raging. Mike picked up a rock with his maw and smashed it into Moriarty's skull, battering him again and again, feeling his own teeth breaking off and not caring. *You can't stop, can you?* Mike roared at his opponent. *Not until you're made to stop.*

Finally, the giant rex sagged beneath him. Mike backed away, horrified, and let the stone fall from his mouth. Moriarty rose. He was shaky, his eyes glazed, but there was still fight in him.

Mike eyed the edge of the cliff. It was a long way

down, even if it was just to the plateau.

Bertram and Candayce had been right, some things were unavoidable—fate.

"What do you say, Professor? It's not the Reichenbach Falls, but...*Wanna flip a coin?*"

Moriarty launched himself at Mike. Mike hugged him close and yanked him to the edge of the cliff. They stumbled, striking the floor of the ledge, and the fragile rock beneath them shattered!

They fell, the ground reaching up for them as they turned and turned, a ten-ton coin flipping and flailing with biting teeth and ripping claws—

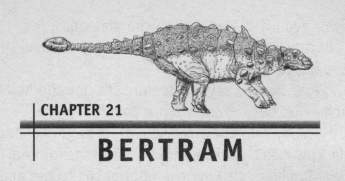

CHAPTER 21

BERTRAM

Bertram saw it all. Janine fell from the cliff, her wings spreading, a current guiding her to an awkward landing. She walked away on shaking legs before collapsing. And above, at the apex of the mountain, Mike and Moriarty battled, then fell over the brink.

Candayce screamed as they dropped, disappearing into the shadows at the far edge of the plateau. A horrible explosion shook the ground.

Another crackling sounded from above. Bertram looked up and saw the mountain shuddering. Rocks bulleted their way.

"Beanie!" Bertram yelled. Then came the explosive force, rocks striking, screams, clumps of dirt and stone, and—an ending. Bertram tried to move, but he was pinned. He'd been buried alive by the rockfall!

He felt a sudden, unexpected impact. The rocks holding him fell away. He looked up to see Beanie staring at him with wide, fear-stricken eyes. He went to her, looking to see if she was hurt. Then he nuzzled

her, and soon her moans died away.

"Candayce!" he yelled. "Janine!"

"Present," came a weak voice from the other side of the pile of rocks. Candayce wobbled toward him on all fours, her pudgy parrot-headed body looking banged up, but functioning.

"Janine?" Candayce yelled. *"Janine!"*

Bertram prayed that she'd taken wing at the last moment, but there was no sound from above.

"We have to find her. Come on!" Bertram said.

He and Candayce dug frantically until they found Janine. She'd been beaten by the rocks, but had managed to avoid the worst of them.

Suddenly, a single, thundering footstep sounded. A tall figure broke from the shadows and fell onto its side. A rex. He was cloaked too firmly in shadows for Bertram or Candayce to identify him.

Candayce wobbled forward, Bertram keeping pace. She stopped before the T. rex. "It isn't Mike."

Bertram came closer. He watched as the last shuddering breath left the giant.

Candayce nudged the giant rex's inert form. "He's dead," she whispered. "Do you think Mike is, too?"

A *caw* sounded from above. Bertram looked up to see Loki glide their way. He dove into the waiting shadows. Another T. rex was lying there.

"Get away!" Bertram screamed. "Leave him alone!"

Candayce launched herself into the shadows. "Shoo! Get away! I'll kick your scaly backside!"

Then silence. Bertram scrambled into the darkness. He saw Loki sitting on a rock beside Mike's still form. Candayce looked over her shoulder, tears in her eyes. "He—he's..."

Snoring, Bertram realized. Mike was *snoring!* Candayce nudged and butted Mike's flank. "Wake up!"

Mike's tiny arms flailed.

"How do you tickle a T. rex?" Candayce asked.

Mike rolled over, and Candayce leaped out of the

way. His eyes opened. "Oh, man. I can't find one part of me that doesn't hurt."

He rolled onto his belly, then tried to rise. He fell back with a loud *crash!*

"Mike, are your legs broken?" Bertram asked.

Mike shook his head. "Everything's spinning. Hold on."

"Take all the time you need," Bertram said.

Soon, Mike rose, tail behind him, chest heaving.

"Bertram," Mike said. "What you were telling me. About Sean. I see it now. I know what to do."

"Good," Bertram said. "I—"

"Bertram!"

Bertram turned to see Janine at the edge of the shadows.

"You'd better come *quick!*" Janine cried. "The M.I.N.D. Machine. It's starting to fade!"

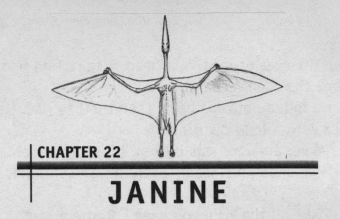

CHAPTER 22

JANINE

Janine saw Mike and Bertram hurry out of the shadows. The machine hung to one side of the rocks that had fallen from the tip of the mountain. Janine could see through its transparent form. Candayce reached the machine first and cried, "What do we do?"

"Do?" Bertram asked.

"To go home!"

"I honestly don't know. Touch it, I guess."

Candayce went to the machine. "Here goes."

She walked right into the machine—and came out the other side.

"It's too late!" Candayce wailed. "We're stuck here!"

"Calm down!" Janine snapped. "Maybe it's what Bertram said. It's got to be all four of us at once."

"Yeah, only you don't *want* to leave," Candayce said. She plopped down on the ground, her head fell to her chest, and she wept. "I wanna go to the mall! I wanna eat things that are really bad for me! I wanna sit in front of the television!"

"There's another problem," Bertram said. "I can't go back, either."

Mike swiveled his head. *"What?"*

Bertram shifted his gaze to Beanie. "She's already lost one mate. I can't do that to her."

"Bertram, she's a dinosaur!" Mike roared.

"So are we."

"It's not the same..."

"No," Bertram said, "it's not. But it means the same to me. I won't do that to her."

"What about us?" Mike asked. *"We* don't want to stay here. Well, Candayce and I don't, anyway."

"Try the machine."

Mike and Candayce walked all around the machine. Nothing. Janine looked at Loki, then at Bertram. "It really is gonna take all four of us."

"I can't do that to Beanie," Bertram said.

Janine was astounded. *She* was the one who was supposed to let everyone down.

Loki tapped her beak with his and studied her. For the first time, Janine knew what it was to be on the other side, with someone looking into *her,* looking deep and uncovering each and every one of her secrets.

Stepping back, Loki cawed, then took a running leap, dove into a thermal, and was carried into the skies.

Janine watched him go. "I think I...just changed my mind. Or I had my mind changed for me."

"What are you babbling about?" Candayce said.

"It's not right, my being here. It's not right for any of us." She looked at Bertram. "She'll be all right."

Bertram shook his head.

"Listen," she said, "all four of us—we've been changed. What's inside these bodies—the spirits, souls of the dinos that were here before us—"

"You're not a dinosaur," Bertram said. "Common misconception. A Quetzalcoatlus—"

"Stop!" Candayce said. "I want to hear this."

"Thank you," Janine said. "We've all been changed. Not just by what we've been through, but by the beings who were inside these bodies before us."

"And they've been changed by us," Bertram said.

"Yes. When we're gone, Beanie will still have a mate. Look inside and tell me I'm not right."

Bertram looked at Beanie, then nuzzled her. "All right. We go. But I'm going to miss her."

"You're serious?" Candayce asked.

Bertram nodded. "She's the only one who ever gave to me without asking for something back."

"She can't *talk*," Candayce said.

Mike whacked Candayce with his tail. "Hush."

"She accepted me as I am," Bertram continued, "and she made me feel stronger than anyone or anything I've ever known. This is my loss, going back. But I know you're right. I don't know how to give her everything I'd want to. Maybe I could learn in time, maybe not. The fact is, we don't belong here...but it *was* a great place to visit."

All four stood beside the machine. They walked into it together—and came out the other side. Nothing had changed.

"All that and it still didn't work?" Janine stared at the machine. "What do you *want,* anyway?"

Bertram's eyes opened wide. "Wait a minute," he said softly. "I think I know."

CHAPTER 23

BERTRAM

"The monitors," Bertram said anxiously. "I just noticed there's an image on them. It's faint. Mike, can you get close enough to see what it is?"

Mike peered into one of the many computer monitor screens on the phantom M.I.N.D. Machine. "It's a bunch of rocks. Weird-looking."

"How many?" Bertram asked excitedly.

"Seven."

"The Standing Stones!" Bertram said. He looked at the pile of rocks that had fallen from above.

Mr. London's words came to him. *Remember, everyone, these folks out there telling you there's nothing new, everything's been done? They're full of it. A hundred years ago, people didn't have skateboards, CDs, or video games. Use your imagination. It's the old saying—*

"If it didn't exist, someone would have to invent it," Bertram said. "We have to *make* the stones!"

"What?" Mike asked. "How?"

Candayce trembled. "Janine's the artist. She could tell us what to do."

Janine nodded. "It's all there. We just have to move things around and sculpt."

Mike shook his head. "Why—"

"*Why?*" Janine came forward, shaking her great wings. "To prove we were here!"

Candayce started trotting in circles. "Janine, every rotten thing I've ever said about you or might say about you, I take back!"

"*Might* say?"

"Let's be realistic."

Janine laughed. "Okay."

Bertram shuddered. "What kind of proof can we leave that won't end up throwing our future into chaos?"

"It's proof for *us*," Mike said. "No one would ever believe it."

"That's true," Janine said. "I can't see the scientific community accepting anything we leave as valid proof of time travel. It would just be looked on as some kind of hoax. Another Bigfoot."

"With my dad at the center," Bertram said glumly.

"What your dad's going to be at the center of is finding that guy." Mike pointed to Moriarty.

Bertram's eyes lit up. "The giant rex! The one he mentioned in the note he left me!"

"I think I know how to make everyone happy," Janine said.

They got to work. The day wore on, and the M.I.N.D. Machine faded a little more as the hours stretched away. Mike helped to clear rock. Janine directed Bertram where to smash the larger rocks. Candayce worked to chisel the stones into seven distinct forms.

The sun was reaching its zenith, and the M.I.N.D. Machine was becoming harder to see.

"We're not gonna make it," Mike said.

"Don't be such an Eeyore," Bertram said. "We'll make it fine."

"If you say so."

Soon, the seven forms were nearly completed. Mike looked at them. "If you stare at these things long enough, some of them look like us!"

"It *is* the four of us," Janine said. "Plus Loki, Beanie, and Moriarty."

"Cool!" Mike said.

"It's something to prove we were here." Janine scratched something into the base of a rock.

"What's that?" Bertram asked.

"My tag. Changed a little."

"I want one!" Candayce said.

Janine fashioned symbols for all seven. Then she sighed. "We did it."

Mike studied the image in the monitor and the stones themselves. "Looks pretty close, anyway."

"It *can't* be perfect," Bertram said. "The elements, sixty-seven million years..."

"So what do we do now?"

Everyone looked at Bertram. "We go back through the machine."

"Are you sure?" Mike asked.

"Yeah. I can feel it this time."

Mike looked over to Moriarty. "Sorry it had to be like this. And that it's all gotta happen again. But there's no other way."

The fallen rex gave no reply.

Bertram felt guilty at having heard those very private words. He went to Candayce, who was staring at the dwindling sun.

"It is pretty, isn't it?" she asked. "Somehow I never noticed."

Janine looked Bertram's way. "Forgot something!"

She raced to the Standing Stones, then came back. Bertram's stomach tightened. "What'd you do?"

Janine held up her chain. "Good luck. We need all we can get right now."

Bertram relaxed.

Janine looked at the sky. "Man, I wish there was time for me to fly again."

Candayce smiled. "You'll fly again."

"What are you talking about?"

"You'll see."

Bertram looked back at Beanie. She was staring at him so fearfully that he wondered if he was making a mistake. He hoped the Ankylosaurus who would soon take over this body again would treat her well. "He'd better, or I'll build another machine."

Beanie angled her head questioningly.

Suddenly, three shapes leaped over the rim and ran toward them. "Ook!" "Eek!" "Ack!"

"Ookeekack!"

Beanie turned to face them. She slammed her tail on the ground, and the Pachys fell. Beanie looked toward Bertram. She was beaming.

He smiled as a fireball of warmth drifted from him to the club-tail. He received one in return.

"Now," Bertram said.

Together, they walked into the phantom machine.

Lightning struck all around them. Unbelievable energies lifted Bertram up, pulling him away from his heavy Ankylosaurus body. For a moment, he felt lighter than he'd ever felt. Below, he saw something—a cyclone—and at its mouth—

A ferocious T. rex approached a pair of Ankylosaurus. The two banded together, smashing at his legs, driving him back. A Leptoceratops ran away, unnoticed by the predator, and a Quetzalcoatlus went to the rim of the plateau and leaped into the sky.

Three dome-shaped heads peered into the wind tunnel, obscuring Bertram's view. Any sounds they might have made were lost in the thunder and crackling forks of energy that blinded him and—

Dropped him to the floor. Hard. Bertram Phillips saw tendrils of lightning vanish from his hands—

His *hands!*

The world was an out-of-focus swirl of activity and voices. How strange—voices that didn't belong to Mike and Candayce and Janine!

He'd made it. He was home!

"Bertram!" Mr. London dropped to his knees beside the thirteen-year-old. "Are you all right?"

Bertram grasped at the glasses Mr. London offered. He slid them on and saw a sea of worried, curious faces. He was back in his own body his own time, and the science fair was still going on.

He heard the M.I.N.D. Machine rocking with life.

"Hey, the geek fried himself. Cool!"

"Mr. Leonitti, consider yourself on report!" Mr. London shouted. "The next person who says anything like that will get the same!"

Bertram was barely listening. He was so...puny. And these clothes he wore felt so unnatural. Where were his spikes? His tail? Where was his *dad?*

A flicker of electricity struck from behind him.

"I have to turn this off!" Mr. London said.

"No!" Bertram said, grabbing the man's arm. "Don't touch it. Cut the power supply."

"Right," Mr. London said.

He disappeared around the side of the machine.

Bertram recalled the blurry shape he'd seen just before his machine carried him away. He had thought it was his dad, but he didn't see his father.

A man pushed his way out of the crowd. "Janine Farehouse! I know she's the cause of this!"

Bertram sighed. It was only Mr. Graves, the teacher who'd been getting on Janine about something that morning.

Janine! Two students were helping her to her feet. About a dozen were clustered around Candayce.

What about Mike? Bertram ran to the window. He saw Mike being helped to his feet on the playing field. A dozen guys were out there now. Mike approached the tallest of them—Sean—and began shouting. Then he turned and shouted at his teammates. Bertram understood what was happening. Mike was making them choose.

Bertram watched as one by one, the players lined up beside Mike.

Sean waved his fists in the air. He looked as if he was screaming. Then he turned and ran.

Score one for evolution, thought Bertram. He looked away, smiling.

It felt a little dizzying standing upright after all those days as a club-tail. He looked at Candayce, who was coming his way. She was beautiful. She glided toward him effortlessly, as if she hadn't been trapped in the body of a Leptoceratops for the last week. Had it really happened? Or had he just—

"Bertram," Candayce said. "Bertram Phillips."

"I—"

Candayce was on him then, one hand around the back of his head, her lips drawing near—

I didn't make it back at all, I'm still dreaming!

She kissed him.

It was the sweetest kiss of his life.

A hush fell upon the crowd. A stunned silence.

Candayce murmured in pleasure, and they both relaxed. It had not been a dream.

Finally, their lips parted.

Bertram's heart was racing. Candayce grinned. This time he kissed her.

"THAT'S MY SON!"

Bertram whirled to face the disbelieving crowd. A man stood at the back, wearing a goofy fishing hat, a brown vest, jeans, and sneakers. His face was covered in fuzz. His cheeks were bright red, but he couldn't stop smiling.

"Dad!" Bertram cried.

Cha-ching!

Bertram and Candayce turned. Janine whipped her key chain. "The mall. Four o'clock. I'll tell Mike."

"Janine, you look good," Candayce said, tears welling up in her eyes. Her voice caught.

Murmurs rose from the crowd.

"Did you *see* that?"

"Bertram Phillips?"

"Where'd he learn to kiss like that?"

Suddenly, lightning crackled behind them. They whirled to see the machine firing up, images playing on its screen.

"The Pachys," Bertram said. Suddenly, three guys leaped from the crowd onto a table and started yelling, "Ook!" "Eek!" "Ack!"

One head-butted another. They looked around the room frantically. Then, with a sizzle, the power faded, and all three guys shook their heads and looked around in confusion as the crowd erupted with laughter.

"What are we doing?" one asked.

Bertram saw Mr. London come around the machine. "It was harder to kill the power than I thought. I had to get insulated gloves."

Bertram squeezed Candayce's hand, then broke from her and went to the machine.

"Bertram!" Janine said breathlessly.

"Be careful," Candayce said.

Taking a deep breath, Bertram reached up and touched the side of the M.I.N.D. Machine. His fingers closed over a handful of circuitry boards. He yanked them off and stuck them in his pocket.

"That ought to do it," he said.

His dad looked to Bertram, Candayce, Janine, then back to his son. "So what'd I miss?"

Bertram just smiled—and hugged his father tight.

CHAPTER 24

MIKE

Eight months later

Mike went outside to pick up the mail. It was a perfect spring day. Bright and sunny with a mild breeze. A moving van went by, and he saw someone looking his way from the cab's passenger seat.

Sean. He didn't wave. Mike watched until the truck reached the end of the street, then made a left and vanished from view.

Mike heard footsteps. He turned to see Bertram, wearing a bulky work shirt.

"Was that who I thought it was?" Bertram asked.

"Yep."

Mike put his hands in his pockets as he walked back to the front door. "It's funny. You think you know someone. You think people will never change. But everyone changes."

Bertram nodded.

They went inside Mike's house. After dropping the

mail on the kitchen table, he went with Bertram to the rec room. There was a TV with a VCR, a couch, and boxes of stuff piled up in the corners.

Candayce and Janine were already there. Glasses of iced tea sat on the small table in front of them. Mike snagged one.

"Oh, look. They're back," Candayce said.

Janine grinned. "I was beginning to think they'd ended up in the Triassic this time."

Bertram peeled off his work shirt, revealing a trimmer, and more muscular, torso. He wore a tight ribbed T-shirt, designer jeans, and boots. He fished out a pair of weights and sat down in a small chair with them, curling without a second thought.

"You better watch it," Mike said. "They're gonna be after you for the wrestling team next."

"Baseball's enough for now," Bertram said.

Janine and Candayce sat on either side of Mike on the couch. Candayce ruffled his hair. "Well? Are you going to keep us in suspense?"

Mike reached for a remote control. "I've finished the scrapbook."

Janine leaped to the edge of the couch. "Lemme see! Lemme see!"

Mike handed her the remote. Janine hit PLAY as Mike turned off the lights.

The TV screen lit up. Mike appeared, holding a microphone. He stood in a crowded hall at school.

"Here we are, back at Wetherford Junior High, and a couple of things have changed."

The image shifted to reveal Bertram at his locker, an uninterested and sad expression on his face as four good-looking young women crowded around him. He seemed lost in a memory.

"Come on!" a young African-American girl said. "You said you'd think about which of us you'd take to the dance."

"I just don't know if I'd really be good company," Bertram said.

Candayce walked by. She laughed, "I had him first!"

"You wish," another girl said.

"It's true." Candayce shrugged.

Bertram nodded. "Yep."

Candayce grinned triumphantly. "See? See?"

"It's all her fault. Get her!"

The camera swung away as the girls chased after Candayce, who laughed and laughed.

"You're so bad," Bertram said.

On the screen, Janine yelled, "Yo, Candy Striper!"

Candayce turned in her red-striped volunteer's uniform. She giggled and shook her head.

Sitting next to Mike, the Candayce of the present put her hand over her face and giggled, too.

The screen cut to a wicked shot from a cliffside. Then it swung over to show Janine, standing under the great wing of a hang glider. She drew a deep breath. "Here I go!" she called.

She ran to the edge and leaped. The camera followed her as she soared down into the valley, screaming with delight.

The images cut to a baseball game, Bertram at the plate. His first swing was a strike. His second connected, and the ball was hit past the outfield.

"Home run!" a voice shouted as Bertram rounded the bases.

"I told you," Mike said, reaching over and shaking Bertram's leg. "See? What'd I tell you?"

The TV cut to an image of Janine at the arts fair, her mom standing proudly behind her as she held up her third-place ribbon for her sculptures.

"Hey," said Janine. "Where's the part I shot for you?"

"It's coming up," said Mike.

The football field appeared with shots of Mike as quarterback in the last game of the season. He let fly a long pass, and the winning touchdown was caught and scored by the smallest member of the team.

"Looks like Lowell finished the season pretty well, didn't he?" asked Bertram.

Mike smiled, looking at images of Lowell being hoisted on his teammates' shoulders. "He sure did."

The video scrapbook played on.

When it was finished and all four had gone upstairs, Mike walked in on Bertram and Janine.

"You did *what?*" Bertram asked.

"I've been meaning to tell you," Janine said, averting her gaze. "I just sort of had to..."

Bertram ran his hand through his hair.

"Hey, that's a trademark move," Mike said. "Watch it."

Smiling sadly, Bertram relayed what Janine had just told him.

"Whoa," Mike said. "Well, you'll just have to talk to your dad. Make sure it's him who comes across it."

"I guess so," Bertram said. "I guess so..."

CHAPTER 25

BERTRAM

Bertram sat at the edge of a small pit with his father. The Standing Stones rose up before them.

"I know I've said it before," his dad muttered, "but I really don't see the point of all this."

"Then I guess I'd better show you." Bertram climbed into the pit and knelt before Janine's stone. The odd symbol she had carved was barely visible. Its lowest reaches were still hidden.

"There's two things we have to go over," Bertram said as he started chipping at the stone.

"Bertram, don't!"

"Relax, Dad. I know what I'm doing. You're not going to find any giant rex bones this close to the stones. Take my word for it."

His father climbed into the pit with him.

"First up," Bertram said, "we need to talk about the household chores and responsibilities."

"Do we have to?" his dad asked in a low voice.

"Yes, we have to. Now, I'll admit, things have been

161

better since the find, the book deal, all that. But lately, you've been slacking off. Last week I had to do the laundry, the cooking, *and* the bills."

"I know. I got swamped."

Bertram chipped away. "I understand. But I have a social life now. Things to do. Responsibilities."

"You're right. I'll be better. I promise."

"Good..." Bertram saw the rock beneath him crack open. "The other thing is the story I told you. About my going back to the Late Cretaceous with Mike and Candayce and Janine—the one you don't believe." Bertram smiled.

"Bertram," his dad said sternly.

"You've had security out here twenty-four hours a day. I tried to get in and couldn't. Neither could my friends. That's what made this necessary."

"I don't see—"

"This whole layer of rock wasn't even excavated until last fall, right? Just before the freeze."

"Yes."

"And today is the first day you've reopened the site. So there's no chance of tampering."

"None."

Bertram stood away from the cracked rock. "Read it, Dad."

His father stared at the rock. He began sputtering. "I—I—"

Bertram nodded. Beneath her tag, Janine had scrawled two words: WAS HERE.

"English," his father whispered. "But that's impossible, unless..."

"Yep," Bertram said. He picked up half the stone and smashed it against the writing.

"Bertram!"

Ignoring his dad, Bertram destroyed the fragile layer of rock in which Janine had made her mark.

"How about we keep it our little secret?" Bertram asked.

"But—but—the information you must have in your head! We need to talk about it. We need—"

"We need to rent a movie."

"What?"

"We need to sit back, have some popcorn, watch some stupid flicks, and have some fun. I need that. What about you?"

Bertram's dad looked down at the rocks.

Bertram put his hand on his dad's shoulder. "It's the past. It's not going anywhere. But in a couple of years, we're going to be talking about college for me, and you could be on a dig who knows where."

Bertram watched as his father stared at the fragments of stone. The older man started to climb from the pit. Bertram followed.

They stood before the Standing Stones as the sun hung low in the sky.

"A movie?" his dad asked. "Have any ideas?"

"Nope. Do you?"

His dad put his arm around him. "Seven stones.

How about *The Magnificent Seven?*"

Bertram took one last look at the stones. "You're on!"

For the first time since he was a little kid, Bertram held his dad's hand as they walked away.

And his dad held *his*.

MR. LONDON

Bob London sat in the basement of Wetherford Junior High, staring at the M.I.N.D. Machine. He'd sworn to Bertram that it had been dismantled, but he couldn't bring himself to do it.

There was something *unusual* about this machine.

For months after the science fair, Mr. London had been unable to sleep. All he could think about was the machine. It couldn't have done half the things he'd seen it do.

Yet he knew what he'd seen. Dead computer monitors flaring to life. Images upon them that resided nowhere on the CD-ROM Bertram had written. Inexplicable energies rising out of the machine's depths.

There were, of course, the circuit boards Bertram had taken from the machine the day of the accident. But it didn't seem reasonable that those boards could have made any real difference.

Mr. London had soldered other boards into the

machine. He'd powered it up and run tests, but all that occurred were the functions it'd been designed to perform.

Mr. London heard the sound of hundreds of feet. It was Friday, and the kids were excited about their weekend.

Maybe on the day of the fair, *he'd* been struck by the electrical impulses, too. They could have messed with his memories, scrambled his perceptions.

Suddenly, a crackling came from all around. Mr. London looked at the machine. It was off. Unplugged.

Lightning whipped about him. He heard a voice.

"You must listen to me. My name is Robert London. I am you some sixty years into what you consider the future. I'm sending this message because I don't know if the one I've sent to Bertram in the Late Cretaceous has reached him or not. If I've failed, then you're their only hope of making it back!"

Mr. London clutched his head as the lightning struck him, filling his mind with schematics, advanced knowledge, and theories.

Then it stopped. The crackling faded.

He looked at the M.I.N.D. Machine again. It was simple now. He understood it. The genius of it. The *power.*

His hands trembled as he plugged in the machine. It would be better, of course, with the circuit boards Bertram had taken, but the replacements he'd installed would serve.

Mr. London activated the program and keyed in dozens of strange sequences. He placed the sensors on his forehead and considered the possibilities.

A door opened. "Mr. London?"

Students. Mr. London stared in shock as a group of them skipped down the stairs.

A boy said, "Mr. Graves sent us. You're supposed to take over study hall for him, and—"

The students froze. Mr. London turned, and his hand mashed the keyboard. The machine roared!

The age of dinosaurs, why did Bertram choose the age of dinosaurs—?

Lightning shot from his hands. It encircled the group of students—and rocketed upward, toward the ceiling! There were screams. Blinding lights!

Mr. London felt himself falling away from his body. He'd done something wrong. He knew it! He reached for the keyboard, but his hand passed through it. Then he was yanked into a cyclone of energies beyond all reason.

From somewhere, he heard the sound of thunder, of ancient roars, of primal creatures that roamed the earth long before the age of man. The screams of the students he'd dragged with him echoed in his mind, then were swallowed up by the howling, incessant winds.

Mr. London cried, "Bertram! *Helllllllllllllp! Berrrrrr-traaaaaam!*"

Then...he was gone.

And the M.I.N.D. Machine sat roaring and raining lightning around the darkened basement.

Waiting.

In a classroom three stories above, Bertram Phillips was overcome by the urge to run down to the basement and see what was wrong.

What could be wrong?

Suddenly, screams. Crackling energies.

Tendrils of light burst up from the floor. They struck two students ahead of him, a boy and a girl. They shouted, then sank to the floor. Others screamed.

Bertram saw more tendrils approaching. Then—

The power cut out. The lightning vanished.

"What happened?" someone asked.

Bertram ran from the classroom and rocketed down the stairs, one flight after another.

Somehow, he already knew.

The journey was over. But the adventure had just begun.

THE ADVENTURE CONTINUES IN

#3

RAPTOR WITHOUT A CAUSE

Oklahoma
112 Million Years Ago

Feeding frenzy!

Will was starved. All he could think about was food, food, *food!*

He was scrambling, clawing, and scratching over the backs of his pals, anxious to get to the grub that was waiting just ahead.

He could smell it—something warm and juicy, a buffet of rich aromas and succulent tastes. His brain was in overdrive.

LEMME AT IT—LEMME AT IT—LEMME AT IT

It took him a moment to really register the sight before him. A dozen lobster-red and neon-green-colored bodies of lean, scaly, nasty raptors were swarming on top of one another like ants. Yipping, snapping, and snarling, they climbed high along the side of a mottled limestone mountain toward their prize.

Little handfuls of dirt and falling rock rushed at their heads, smacked, and bounced off. Terrible claws sliced the air. Razor-lined maws bit like chattering teeth. Bellies rumbled. Tails whacked and whipped out and were stepped on.

Will stood on unsteady legs. He looked down at his hands and saw the same terrible claws the other raptors displayed. On his feet, something clicked and clacked. Retractable crescent moon-shaped hooks, powerful and deadly. Between his hands and feet, he saw a striped rust-colored body with a splash of sky blue snaking around the belly, and powerfully muscled legs.

He shuddered.

"My name is Will Reilly. I am thirteen years old. I am a student at Wetherford Junior High. I like being a student at Wetherford Junior High. I like throwing parties. I like my music. I like being me. Who wouldn't?"

He hesitated.

"Okay, that was a little cocky. True, but cocky."

Will squeezed his hind muscles and felt his tail swoosh from side to side. Chills raced through him. "I don't want to have scales. I don't want to be naked. I don't want to have a tail. No. No way, no how."

His stomach grumbled. A boiling hot desire burned through his brain.

HUNGRY—HUNGRY—HUNGRY—HUNG—

"I don't care if I'm hungry," he hissed. "I don't care what I'm looking at, what I'm smelling, what I'm feeling, I don't care. I am not—"

Something that looked like a rat poked its head out of a small hole near the base of the mountain. Will roared and leaped for it with blinding speed, his jaws chomping, spittle flying everywhere...

#3

RAPTOR WITHOUT A CAUSE
COMING IN MAY 2000!

COMING IN JULY 2000!

#4
PLEASE DON'T EAT THE TEACHER!
by Scott Ciencin

My name is Mr. London and I'm a science teacher. A few hours ago, my main concern was keeping every student's attention on me. Now I'm trying to get one student's attention *off* me. You see, I've become a tiny, two-foot-tall Hypsilophodon, and my least patient student has become a towering, meat-eating Acrocanthosaurus. To her, I look like a tasty chicken nugget. I may be dead meat—unless I can get my newest lesson plan through her hungry head: Don't eat the teacher!

EXTINCTION IS <u>NOT</u> AN OPTION.

BERTRAM'S NOTEBOOK

BERTRAM'S NOTEBOOK

Ankylosaurus (ANG-kih-luh-saw-rus): One of the last armored dinosaurs and largest of the club-tails. Built low to the ground, Ankylosaurus walked on all fours and weighed three to four tons. Even Ankylosaurus's eyelids were armored!

Ankylosaurus

Carnivores (KAR-nuh-vorz): Meat-eating animals.

Cretaceous (krih-TAY-shus): The last of three distinct periods in the Mesozoic Era, 145 million to 65 million years ago.

Crocodilians (krok-uh-DILL-ee-unz): A sizable collection of reptiles that spawned modern crocodiles and other now-extinct creatures, some larger than any carnivorous dinosaur.

Herbivores (HUR-bih-vorz): Plant-eating animals.

Ichthyosaurs (IK-thee-uh-sorz): Water-dwelling, fish-eating, air-breathing reptiles.

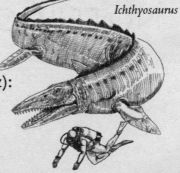

Ichthyosaurus

Invertebrates (in-VUR-tuh-braytz): Animals without backbones, like jellyfish.

Leptoceratops (lep-tuh-SER-uh-tops): The name means "slender-horned face." It was a Protoceratops of the same family as Triceratops. Leptoceratops was distinguished by its smaller size (the size of a pig), absence of horns, and beaked face. Leptoceratops was found only in North America.

Leptoceratops

Mammals (MAM-ulz): In the Cretaceous, they were small hairy animals.

Mesozoic Era (mez-uh-ZOH-ik ER-uh): The age of dinosaurs, 245 million to 65 million years ago.

Pachycephalosaurus (pack-ih-SEF-uh-luh-saw-rus): The name means "thick-headed lizard." These plant-eaters used their domelike heads for defense, ramming opponents with them much like present-day mountain goats.

Pachycephalosaurus

Paleontologist (pay-lee-un-TAHL-uh-jist): A scientist who studies the past through fossils.

Parasaurolophus (par-uh-saw-ruh-LOH-fus): Plant-eating crested dinosaur that was thirty feet long and stood sixteen feet high. Parasaurolophus' crest was a long, hornlike tube that curved backward from the head to beyond the shoulders and produced sounds.

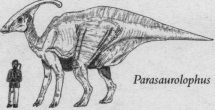

Parasaurolophus

Protoungulatums (proh-toh-UNG-gyuh-lah-tumz): Tiny mammals that were the forerunners of horses, antelopes, camels, and so on. They appeared to be part cat, part rat, and part horse.

Pterosaurs (TER-uh-sorz): Sizable and varied flying reptiles.

Quetzalcoatlus (ket-sahl-koh-AHT-lus): A pterosaur, a flying reptile that was not actually a dinosaur. A full-grown Quetzalcoatlus had a thirty-six- to thirty-nine-foot wingspan. It was the largest flying creature of all time.

Quetzalcoatlus

Triceratops (try-SER-uh-tops): "Three-horned face." Triceratops weighed up to eleven tons and traveled in great herds near the end of the Late Cretaceous period in North America.

Triceratops

Tyrannosaurus rex (ty-RAN-uh-saw-rus recks): "King of the tyrant lizards," a large meat-eating dinosaur with tiny but enormously powerful arms and muscular jaws filled with fifty teeth. Paleontologists differ on whether the T. rex was a predator who attacked live prey, a scavenger who lived on carcasses, or both.

Tyrannosaurus rex

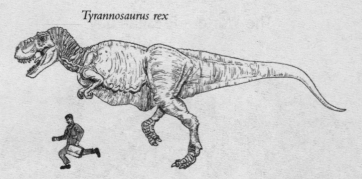

Vertebrates (VUR-tuh-braytz): Animals with backbones, like fish, mammals, reptiles, and birds.

The world: The continents and the seas of the earth 67 million years ago were different from those in our present day. North America was subdivided by an inland sea, and water also prevented movement between North and South America. Mexico was under water, India was a separate island, South America and Africa had begun to separate, and Europe and North America were moving apart. Seaways also divided Europe and Asia.

The World—Present Day

The World—67 Million Years Ago

SCOTT'S FAVORITE DINO SITES

(and Bertram has them bookmarked, too!)

DINO RUSS'S LAIR
http://www.isgs.uiuc.edu/dinos/dinos_home.html
A terrific site with lots of dinosaur information, including digs, dinosaur eggs, dino societies, exhibits, books, breaking news, software, and much more.

DINOSAUR ART AND MODELING
http://www.indyrad.iupui.edu/public/jrafert/dinoart.html
A terrific resource for artists and model-makers interested in dinosaurs. Original art by fans is posted on the site.

DINOSAURIA ON-LINE
http://www.dinosauria.com
Your window into the Mesozoic! Articles and discussions from enthusiasts and actual paleontologists on various dinosaur topics. Fossil replicas for sale. A dino picture gallery. The Omnipedia—a dinosaur encyclopedia at your fingertips, including maps of the ancient earth, dictionaries, pronunciation guides, and more!

THE PALEO RING
http://www.pitt.edu/~mattf/PaleoRing.html
An ever-evolving assortment of more than two hundred web sites devoted to dinosaurs and paleontology!

THE PARASAUROLOPHUS SOUND HOME PAGE AT THE NEW MEXICO MUSEUM OF NATURAL HISTORY AND SCIENCE
http://www.nmmnh-abq.mus.nm.us/nmmnh/parasound.html
Very cool—listen to the music of these very special dinosaurs!

BOOKS THE AUTHOR READ

Benyus, J. M. *Beastly Behaviors: A Zoo Lover's Companion*. Reading, Mass.: Addison-Wesley, 1992.

Bloch, M. H. *Footprints in the Swamp*. New York: Atheneum, 1985.

Czerkas, S. J., and S. A. Czerkas. *Dinosaurs: A Global View*. New York: Mallard Press, 1991.

Dixon, D. *Dougal Dixon's Dinosaurs*. Honesdale, Pa.: Boyds Mills Press, 1993.

Dixon, D., B. Cox, R. J. G. Savage, and B. Gardiner. *The Macmillan Illustrated Encyclopedia of Dinosaurs and Prehistoric Animals*. New York: Simon & Schuster/Macmillan Company, 1988.

Dodson, P. *An Alphabet of Dinosaurs*. New York: Scholastic, 1995.

Eyewitness Visual Dictionaries. *The Visual Dictionary of Dinosaurs*. New York: Dorling Kindersley, 1993.

Fastovsky, D. E., and D. B. Weishampel. *The Evolution and Extinction of the Dinosaurs*. New York: Cambridge University Press, 1996.

Glut, D. F. *Dinosaurs: The Encyclopedia*. Jefferson, N.C.: McFarland & Company, Inc., 1997.

Hanson, J. K., and D. Morrison. *Of Kinkajous, Capybaras, Horned Beetles, Seladangs, and the Oddest and Most Wonderful Mammals, Insects, Birds, and Plants of Our World*. New York: HarperCollins, 1991.

Horner, J. R., and D. Lessem. *The Complete T. Rex*. New York: Simon & Schuster, 1993.

Lambert, D. *Field Guide to Prehistoric Life*. New York: Facts on File, 1985.

Lambert, D. *The Ultimate Dinosaur Book*. New York: Dorling Kindersley, 1993.

Lambert, D., and Diagram Visual Information Ltd. *The Dinosaur Data Book*. New York: Avon Books, 1990.

Lessem, D. *Dinosaur Worlds*. Honesdale, Pa.: Boyds Mills Press, 1996.

Lessem, D. *Ornithomimids: The Fastest Dinosaur*. Minneapolis: Carolrhoda Books, 1996.

Masson, J. M., and S. McCarthy. *When Elephants Weep: The Emotional Lives of Animals*. New York: Bantam Doubleday Dell, 1995.

Norman, D. *Dinosaur!* New York: Prentice Hall General Reference, 1991.

Norman, D. *The Illustrated Encyclopedia of Dinosaurs*. London: Salamander Books Limited, 1985.

Retallack, G. J. "Pedotype Approach to Cretaceous and Tertiary Paleosols, Montana." *Geological Society of America Bulletin,* 106, no. 11 (1994).

Stanley, S. M. *Earth and Life Through Time*. New York: W. H. Freeman, 1989.

Walker, C., and D. Ward. *The Eyewitness Handbook of Fossils*. New York: Dorling Kindersley, 1992.

Wellnhofer, P. *Pterosaurs: The Illustrated Encyclopedia of Prehistoric Flying Reptiles*. New York: Barnes and Noble Books, 1991.

Wilford, J. N. *Riddle of the Dinosaur*. New York: Knopf, 1985.

• AUTHOR'S SPECIAL THANKS •

Special thanks to Alice Alfonsi, my amazing editor, and all our friends at Random House, especially Kate Klimo, Kristina Peterson, Craig Virden, Kenneth LaFreniere, Georgia Morrissey, Gretchen Schuler, Mike Wortzman, Artie Bennett, and Doby Daenger. Thanks also to Denise Ciencin, M.A., National Certified Counselor, for her many valued and wonderful contributions to this novel. Thanks to Dr. Thomas R. Holtz, Jr., Vertebrate Paleontologist, Department of Geology, University of Maryland, for serving as project adviser, and to my incredible agent, Jonathan Matson.